MELODY
OF LOVE

MELODY
OF LOVE

•

Tara Randel

AVALON BOOKS
NEW YORK

PRINTED IN THE UNITED STATES OF AMERICA
ON ACID-FREE PAPER
BY HADDON CRAFTSMEN, BLOOMSBURG, PENNSYLVANIA

To my brothers,
Bill and Kevin,
with love.

Acknowledgments

To Diana Nicholas, songwriter extraordinaire, for your musical expertise. I appreciate all your help. To Mira, thanks for your insight in making this a special book. To Randy, Megan, and Kathryn, I love you. And to Kim, as usual and always, tons of thanks.

Chapter One

Fat raindrops pelted Marilyn Banner's tired old Cadillac as she turned the key in the ignition. For the sixth time. *Click. Whirr.* Nothing.

"Please," she coaxed. "Just start."

She turned the key yet again. Nothing. Drawing a frustrated breath, she rested her forehead on the chilled steering wheel. Things had gone from bad to worse today. This week. Make it the entire month. She'd lost two deals and her boss was not at all pleased. The national news may have claimed that it was a buyer's market for real estate, but her commissions proved otherwise. She'd made employee of the month in top sales for six months in a row, but the past few weeks had been slow.

Now her usually dependable Cadillac had decided to play fickle. So much for getting home from work at a reasonable hour. She gripped the steering wheel and squeezed hard, tamping down her mounting frustration. She should have listened to her brother, Ty,

1

and taken it in for a tune-up. But she didn't have the time and really hated when Ty was right. Which was way too often lately.

She rested her chin on the wheel, catching a glimpse of a dark figure crossing before the car. Seconds later, a tapping came from the window.

Marilyn jumped, her heart suspended in her chest.

A stranger motioned for her to roll down the window.

Marilyn hesitated. Rain slicked over his drenched Stetson and he squinted to keep the moisture from his eyes. A black oilskin coat protected his clothing from the downpour. He might have been a guardian angel to someone else, but to her he was still a stranger. The fact that she was sitting in her car, downtown, in plain view of everyone, was the only reason she complied.

"Are you okay, ma'am?" came his concerned drawl.

"My car won't start."

"Want me to check it out?"

"Um, I appreciate the gesture, but I, um . . ."

He grinned. "You don't know me from Adam?"

"Yes."

"I can assure you, I have no evil intentions running around in my head. C'mon, even a crazy person wouldn't be out in this rotten weather, let alone help a stranded motorist."

"I'm not exactly stranded. I'm still in the town square."

He looked around the empty square, then flashed her a smile of even white teeth. "Only doing my civic duty."

Marilyn looked at him again, seeing sincerity in his partially hidden eyes. What the heck? After all, it was daylight, even with the gloom hanging over them. If he tried anything funny, she'd scream and lay on the horn. At least she had a plan.

She popped the hood. "Go ahead."

He nodded and jogged over to investigate her engine failure. "Try it again," he yelled.

She turned the key. Not even a click this time.

He dropped the hood and ran back to the window, rivulets of water rushing off the brim of his hat, splashing Marilyn through the open window. "I'm not a mechanic, but I think it's pretty safe to say your battery is dead."

She wiped her face and slumped back into the seat. "Figures."

"I can run into the general store and call for help."

That would have been her next plan, since she knew her cell phone was dead because she'd forgotten to recharge the battery. Besides, she was only half a block from Ben and Molly and the warmth of their general store. They'd have a working phone and fresh hot coffee or cider.

"Thanks, but I think I'll head over there myself." No point in sitting in this useless pile of steel. Marilyn closed the window, grabbed her umbrella and gingerly stepped from the car, her high heels skimming over a stream of rushing water before stepping directly into a deep puddle.

She cringed as cold water seeped into her leather pump. Gritting her teeth, and hanging on to a very short fuse of temper, she slammed the car door. She wondered if the day could get any worse.

After a struggle with the handle of her umbrella, she thumbed the clasp that released the spring, then clutched the lapels of her trench coat and hurried to the sidewalk. "I'll be okay now," Marilyn assured the man.

He held out his hand to assist her. "You sure?"

She ignored the gesture, fuming over the dead car, her helplessness, and this guy's assumption that she needed him. She didn't. Not him or anyone else.

"Look, just let me get you to the store."

He took a few steps closer, his fingers closing over her hand still gripping the umbrella.

"I'll be—"

As Marilyn skirted a puddle, the sole of her shoe slid on a patch of mud. She flailed and the stranger tightened his grasp, trying to dodge the umbrella. They stood suspended, gaping at each other for mere seconds, before Marilyn's ankle gave way. The umbrella bobbed helter-skelter and the man let go to protect Marilyn from the pointed ends extending from the cloth dome about to scratch her face. Marilyn pitched back in slow motion, landing bottom first in the puddle, the umbrella askew and her coat flying wide open.

"Look what you did!" she cried, stunned.

"Hey, I only tried to help."

He bent down to offer his hand. Marilyn batted it away. "I can manage."

She put a hand down in the cold rain runoff, grimaced, and pushed herself up, the puddle water dripping down her legs. In a fit of pique, she yanked her drenched skirt back down to a respectable level, not willing to give this stranger any more entertainment on her account.

She looked up to find him smiling at her. The lines

around his eyes crinkled with humor. "I'm really sorry."

"Oh, sure, I'll bet you are."

"You have to admit, this is kinda funny."

"From your point of view," Marilyn huffed "Do you make a show of helping people before tossing them down to the ground?"

"I didn't toss you, you slipped."

"Right."

His face grew serious and he took a step back, almost as if he was concerned about hanging around too much longer. "If you're really okay . . ."

"I am."

"Then I'll be off." Hesitantly, he took a step toward her. "You sure?"

"Very."

At her clipped answer, he turned on his heel and disappeared before Marilyn could come up with another smart retort. By now her teeth were chattering and her legs were shaking. Where had her umbrella gone to? She spied it, end up, beside the dreaded puddle. With frustration, she grabbed the handle. She could just imagine how awful her hair and makeup must look. She let out a huff and took off for the store, more than ready to be fussed over as soon as she crossed the threshold.

"Anyone here?" she called, shaking out the umbrella and stamping her numb feet. The rich aroma of brewed coffee enveloped her immediately, calming her frayed nerves.

"Be right there," Molly's voice sang from the back of the store.

Marilyn shucked off her raincoat and shook out the last of the moisture. Just as she draped it over an old wooden coat rack, another familiar voice sounded behind her.

"Look who just rolled in from the rain."

Marilyn took a deep breath before turning around to face Kitty Leacock, nemesis extraordinaire. Dressed to the hilt in a designer trench coat, neatly pressed black slacks, and sleek leather boots, along with the prerequisite accessories of a matching hat and umbrella. How did the woman manage to look so put together, so dry, on a day like this?

"Still raining hard, Marilyn?" Kitty smirked. Her gaze drifted over Marilyn's drenched clothes and ruined hair.

"Actually, it's letting up, Kitty." Who named their child Kitty, anyway? At twenty-eight, they should all be calling her Cat.

"As always, it's a thrill to run into you, but I have a meeting with the Library Guild. I'm the new chairman of the building committee." With a precisioned flick of long acrylic fingernails, Kitty tucked her heavily highlighted blond hair under the trendy hat she sported.

"Congratulations." Another title to add to Kitty's list of accomplishments. She'd started her list in high school and had steadily built an impressive resumé of volunteer community work. Widowed last year, Kitty had thrown herself into any charitable work available. Marilyn couldn't blame her. She couldn't imagine being that young and losing her husband.

But Kitty always seemed to rub her success in. The fact that they were both the same age, and Kitty had done so much, never ceased to be a thorn in Marilyn's side. It seemed that every accomplishment she'd attained in school, Kitty made it before her. Kitty came from a respectable family that always had the support of the community. And Kitty never let Marilyn forget what she'd done and Marilyn had not. They'd both strived for good grades in school, but Kitty made the National Honors Society while Marilyn missed it by a point. One lousy point.

Kitty unsnapped her umbrella. "I'm off. Oh, by the way, I'm also heading up the charity scholarship committee this year. Since your grandmother is heading the festival committee, I'm sure we'll cross paths to discuss the recipients and the award ceremonies at the festival."

"I'm sure we will."

"Ta." Kitty wiggled her fingers in what Marilyn thought was a wave.

"Ta."

As soon as Kitty had left, Molly Pike came bustling toward her.

"Mercy, but it's nasty weather out today. And then to have to deal with Kitty." Molly stopped dead. Her eyes grew wide. "What on earth happened to you?"

"I had a close encounter with the sidewalk."

Molly rushed over and draped her arm around Marilyn. "Lord, you must be freezing. Come over here by the fire."

Marilyn shuddered again until the heat pouring from the old Franklin stove warmed through her clothes right to the skin. "I was on my way home but my car died."

"Again? Oh, dear. Ben," she called toward the back of the store. "I need you out here."

Marilyn heard a muffled response.

Molly turned back to Marilyn and grimaced. "You know, if you settled down with a nice man, you wouldn't have to work. Why, your grandmother would be thrilled to see you married."

Marilyn sighed. "Yes, Gran would be thrilled."

Same old song and dance. Since she wasn't seeing anyone romantically, you'd think they'd all have given up on the marriage idea by now. Her grandmother. Molly and Ben. And just about all her grandmother's friends who'd tried playing matchmaker. Marilyn didn't know if she was being overly sensitive, but it seemed that their efforts had doubled over the last year.

She might be single, but her career was speeding along and she had no intention of slowing down. Not for anyone.

"You know," Molly continued, "you could keep your grandmother out of trouble if you settled down."

Marilyn grinned, not exactly convinced by that skewed logic. "Gran would much rather I stay out of her way. She thinks I moved back home to spy on her. Not that she doesn't deserve it."

Molly chuckled, maneuvering around a display of homemade jam as she rounded the corner to the coffeemaker. "Truth be told, I'm glad you've moved in with her. That last stroke really took a lot out of her, although she'd never admit it."

"She's as stubborn as they come. Don't tell her I said this, but I'm happy to be home with her. She's been there for me my entire life. The least I can do is help her out now."

"She's got that beautiful house, but it's much too big for only two women." Molly shook her head and tsked. "All those empty bedrooms and no grandchildren to fill them, except for Emily who lives so far away."

Molly came back around the corner holding a cup of something steaming. Hopefully her famous Paineville cider. Marilyn sighed as she accepted the drink. Some traditions were better than others.

Marilyn walked to the wall across from the counter, catching a glimpse of herself in the old, scarred Coke mirror. She nearly choked at the sight. Her normally stylish blonde hair hung in clumps around her face.

This was that cowboy's fault, she groused silently. Her cheeks stained scarlet at the thought of the stranger. He'd put her in this sorry state, then ran for the hills.

She stepped closer to the mirror to survey the damage, squishy sounds coming from her ruined shoes. Unable to look anymore, she closed her eyes tightly, an image of the cowboy filling her head. *He* had strong, sturdy boots, as she remembered. No doubt he wasn't making strange noises when he walked.

Her eyes flew open, horror reflecting back at her. *Why was she thinking about him?*

"Speaking of that big house," Molly said, thankfully giving Marilyn a reprieve from her wayward thoughts, "I think your grandmother's newest idea makes sense. Should have thought of it years ago."

"I'm sorry, what did you say?" Marilyn asked as she grabbed her purse and fished around for a brush.

"Ruby Sue's idea."

Warning bells clamored in Marilyn's head. She paused in her search. "What idea?"

Molly stared at her. "Why, certainly she's told you?" Her plump hand covered her mouth. "Oh, dear."

"Oh, dear what?"

Molly backed away. "Maybe she should tell you."

Marilyn took a deep breath to control the sudden pounding in her head. Her grandmother's ideas were notorious, usually causing countless family upheavals. "It's a bit too late for you to turn back now, Molly. Besides, I'm used to Ruby Sue's surprises. So tell me, what do you know?"

The round woman's shoulders slumped. "She's taken in a boarder."

A ton of bricks falling on her head couldn't have knocked Marilyn back more. "A what?"

"You know, someone to rent a room and pay your grandmother." Molly's brow creased as she frowned at Marilyn. "Personally I think she was lonely and wanted some company."

"A boarder? She doesn't need anyone. I'm home now."

Molly picked up a box at the end of the counter. "I can't explain your grandmother, dear," she commented before heading to the back room.

Marilyn squeezed her eyes shut. She loved her grandmother, really she did. But sometimes Ruby Sue made her absolutely and completely crazy.

How could her grandmother be lonely? The woman had more of an active social life than Marilyn. Not that Marilyn was home much with her grandmother lately, due to her tight schedule. And right now Marilyn didn't need a guilty reminder of her grueling work hours and not being around for Gran, twenty-four/seven. Part of having financial success were the long hours that went with the job of a real estate agent. She had to be flexible for the clients. Still, Marilyn hated leaving Gran home alone.

But, hey, it was better than when she was growing up poor. Always ignoring the snickers behind her back, kids taunting her because she'd lived in a run-down trailer with her grandmother and brothers so long ago.

Banners never amounted to much and never will.

She frowned as the familiar words echoed in her mind.

It was bad enough that her father had taken off for parts unknown, leaving her broken-hearted mother behind. Eventually her mother grew lonely and restless. In time, the other women in town kept their husbands away from 'that loose woman.' Rumors flew, and her mother's already shaky reputation was tarnished. At the time, Marilyn wasn't old enough to understand those rumors, but she was young enough to feel the aftereffects.

Even here, in the general store, memories slipped into her heart. She remembered, as a little girl, standing at the counter, holding her mother's hand while a woman Marilyn didn't know quite vocally warned her mother to stop speaking to the woman's husband. "And keep your children away from decent folk."

The scene left a lasting impression on Marilyn's young soul. And the result had been that Ben asked Marilyn's mother not to come into the store again. He didn't want any trouble between customers.

Marilyn learned to hide her shame at similar situations, right up until the time her mother left. When she got older, she learned that one of the rumors involved her mother and Kitty's father. Nothing was ever proven, but from that moment on Kitty drew the battle lines.

Never one to play fair, Kitty always managed to rub Marilyn's face in the fact that she didn't live in a fancy house, like Kitty did. Or have two parents at home, like Kitty. Or have all the boys running after her, like Kitty.

Once out of high school, Marilyn worked extra hard and made a successful name for herself, despite her mother's legacy. Nothing would take that away. She was not, and never would be, her mother.

And as many times as she crossed paths with Kitty, she tried not to let that woman's petty claws scratch her. Still, the run-ins smarted from time to time.

Marilyn placed her cup on the aged wood of the store counter and turned to retrieve her coat. She needed to find out what her independent grandmother had in mind with this boarder.

"I need to get home and talk some sense into Gran," Marilyn called out as she shrugged her coat over her shoulders. "Thanks for the coffee."

She had a foot out the door before Molly came back into the store and stopped her. "Dear, your car? It's broken."

Marilyn groaned. Her hands closed in fists. She couldn't go anywhere until someone jump-started her car.

Ben ambled into the store proper, his face breaking into a broad grin as he viewed his customer. "Marilyn, where are you going in such a hurry?"

Resigned to another delay, Marilyn headed for the

phone. "I need to call Hank down at the garage. My car died."

"Why, that's the second time this month."

"Please, don't remind me." Marilyn reached for the old-time receiver on the wall and made the call. Then, just as soon as possible, she'd head home and sort out her grandmother's newest scheme.

By the time Marilyn retrieved her car and started home, the late-afternoon gloom deepened under thick cloud cover. The rain had stopped an hour earlier, leaving the curving mountain road slick with errant leaves fallen from the trees. The temperature was dropping steadily and a rich, earthy scent of wet ground and decaying foliage announced autumn had arrived. Even though she didn't want to dwell on the state of affairs at home, Marilyn allowed a small smile as she drank in the beauty of the North Georgia mountains. This was her favorite time of the year. Harvest. Cold morning air condensing your breath. Sitting in front of a warm fire in the evenings. Ruby Sue's prize-winning pumpkin pie.

Marilyn was born and raised here and had tried for years to overcome her mother's desertion, thinking maybe she should leave in order to build a different life for herself. But as hard as she tried, she never could escape this town. After high school, at her grandmother's urging and after learning it was all she could afford, she decided to go to a local business school. She had grand plans to move away after graduation, but both her brothers, Ty and Gabe, had left Paineville, so she stayed not wanting the older woman to be lonely. She accepted a job here in town and stayed local since.

But now that Ty was home, she could resume with her goal to escape the small town. That translated into long hours at work. Looking into the horizon, wondering what the future might have in store. Only deep in the secret recesses of her heart did she admit how much she loved home. But another part of her wanted to know if she could really be successful on her own. Out there, in the big world.

Which was why the Charlotte offer came as such a welcome surprise.

For the past five years she'd been a top producer in the greater Paineville area real estate game. These past six months she'd dealt with clients from the Charlotte area and they'd been impressed. Impressed enough to recommend her to a major company in the big city. She'd been thrilled about the referrals, hoping this would help in her dream to leave Paineville and work in a bigger market. And then the call had come first thing this morning.

The offer included joining a nationally-recognized real estate group, a raise in her bonuses, and they'd even help her with relocation fees.

How ironic. All the years she'd tried desperately to leave this little town and nothing came her way. With Ruby Sue's questionable health, and now the boarder issue, she gets the job of a lifetime.

Prestige, a raise, and the chance to move to a large city.

But could she take off and leave the woman who raised her? Too bad she couldn't take her grandmother with her, but she knew Ruby Sue would never leave these mountains. She was rooted and grounded here.

Marilyn pulled off the main road and slowly motored the half mile to the house. Desperately, she tried coming up with a solution before she parked the car.

She considered asking her older brother, Ty, to step in and take care of Ruby Sue, but he'd recently gotten married. Ruby Sue would never impose on them. Her other brother, Gabe, lived in Florida. Again, Marilyn knew Ruby Sue would never move, so she already knew the answer to that question.

The white mailbox at the end of the drive signaled the end of Marilyn's musing. After turning up the drive, she slammed on the brakes when she spied a pickup truck parked in her usual spot. It wasn't her brother's truck. Who else would be here at dinnertime?

The boarder. She eased closer before turning off the car. A black, half-ton monster splattered with mud from the earlier rain dwarfed her Caddy. She exited the car, her stomach squeezed into a painful knot at the enormity of her grandmother's actions. She slowly walked around the truck to check the tag. Tennessee. Did they know anyone from that state?

Suddenly, terrible thoughts assailed her. What if this person was using their house to hide out from the law? Or maybe to rob them? Ruby Sue was tough, but she could be pretty trusting at times.

Her stomach still clenched, Marilyn savagely unzipped her purse, hunting through the mess to find her antacids. She wanted to be prepared before whatever . . . faced her inside.

Her search came up empty. With dismay, she realized she'd left the roll at the office.

Lifting her head, she plodded forward, determined not to lose her temper and not mention her offer in Charlotte.

Yet.

The lovely Victorian-style house with the grand porch, complete with rocking chairs and a swing, greeted her like an old friend. Her brother had lovingly built this house as a gift to their grandmother, and he'd hired the best craftsmen from miles around to do the perfect job. It showed in the gingerbread-lattice detail nestled in the corners of the porch ceiling, to the stenciled shutters and glass-etched front door.

Marilyn quietly entered the foyer, hanging her coat on a peg in the hallway and setting her purse on the mahogany hall table, smiling as the delicious aroma of Ruby Sue's pot roast wafted toward her from the kitchen. She breathed deeply and strode into the living room, only to stop short at the scene before her.

A man sat in a large wing-backed chair, his profile angled toward the fireplace. He rested his elbows on the arms of the chair, his hands steepled beneath his chin, apparently deep in thought. In the light of the fire, she noticed a slight frown as he studied the mesmerizing flames crackling before him.

Marilyn's stomach dipped with recognition.

He sensed her arrival, and his gaze tore from the jumping flames to pierce her eyes with his.

She would have recognized him anywhere. Dry now, his chestnut-hued hair gleamed in the ambient light. He wore a flannel shirt, faded blue jeans and dark work boots. Slowly, he rose from the chair to his full six-foot height, his eyebrows raised in what she could only assume was surprise in his laughing blue eyes.

She certainly hadn't expect to see the stranger who had dumped her into a puddle seated comfortably in her grandmother's living room. And judging by his look, he hadn't expected to see her either.

"Guess your car's fixed," he said, the slow drawl she'd heard earlier still evident in his speech.

"Yes."

"The battery?"

"Needed a jump."

He stuffed a hand into his front jeans pocket. "Time to get a new one?"

"This one will do for now."

His lips pulled up just a touch at the corners. If she didn't know better, she'd think he was enjoying her surprise.

"What are you doing here?" she demanded.

"Joining Ruby Sue for dinner."

She paused for a moment, then made the plunge. "*Who* are you?"

"Your grandmother's new boarder." He smiled. A smile slow and full of secrets. "Pleased to meet you, ma'am."

Chapter Two

"Name's Dusty Haywood."

He held out his hand, sensing she wouldn't take it. He knew he shouldn't be yanking the chain of the uptight, yet very pretty, woman standing before him, but he couldn't help it. Her eyebrows arched all serious-like, and her hands were opening and closing into tightly bunched fists. If he didn't know better, he'd think that cute blush across her cheeks had more to do with his presence and less with her indignation. Because here he was, in her domain, and she didn't like it.

No surprise here.

He had answered the ad for a boarder, needing a place to stay while he figured out his next career move. He'd liked Ruby Sue the minute he spoke to her when he'd called to inquire. And that was before he saw the house. Now, standing in the cozy living room and waiting for what smelled like one mighty fine dinner, he had no intentions of leaving anytime soon.

Regardless of the fuming woman standing in the doorway, no matter how lovely she looked.

"Just when did you move in?" she asked.

"A few hours ago. Got the first bedroom, upstairs to the left."

"And how long do you plan on staying?"

Dusty dropped his hand. "As long as it takes."

"To do what?"

"Figure out my plan."

The woman's eyebrows rose higher in surprise. Guess she hadn't expected that answer.

"So, who're you?" he asked in the same tone she used in her fifth-degree questioning.

"That would be my granddaughter, Marilyn," Ruby Sue announced as she entered the dining room carrying a steaming platter of meat and vegetables, an orange tabby cat dancing at her heels. She set it down before joining them in the living room. "You know, the other boarder here. The one who doesn't make decisions for me. The one who works most of the time anyway."

Dusty turned his gaze to Marilyn, eager to hear her response.

"Gran, not now."

"Why not? This is my house and I can pick the conversation."

"Not in front of the stranger—I mean, *boarder*."

Dusty grinned. All flustered like this, Marilyn seemed vulnerable. He found he liked that.

"Don't matter much who I talk in front of. You don't listen anyway. Now let's sit down to dinner."

Uh-oh. Sounded like a recurring argument to him. The trio crossed into the dining room to take a seat at the table, the women glaring at each other. Just his luck, the platter of pot roast and potatoes at his elbow and he was too polite to eat until the ladies called a truce.

"Marilyn, for heaven's sake, what happened to your clothes?"

She stared pointedly at Dusty. "I had a little accident in town."

"You okay?"

"Yes, I'm fine. My outfit, however, is less than fortunate."

"Why don't you change your clothes before we eat dinner?"

Marilyn nodded to her grandmother and glared at Dusty. "This isn't over with you either," she told him as she passed by. Her subtle perfume trailed behind her as she left the room, leaving the lingering scent of . . . Joy? Judging by his past experience with women, it sure smelled elegant to him.

"Don't mind her," Ruby Sue said as she dished out the meal. "I didn't tell her my plans to find a boarder so this comes as a surprise."

"I guessed that."

"She's a good girl—just got her life focused on the wrong things."

"At least she has a focus."

"You don't strike me as the sort of man who's floundering around in life."

"Not normally, just the past few months. I'm sort of at a crossroads." Ready to change the subject, Dusty took a bite of the savory meat and groaned out loud. "I haven't had good home cooking in years. If you promise this kind of food every night, I'll be a permanent boarder."

Ruby Sue grinned. "Don't make promises you can't keep."

Dusty lifted his fork, ready for another mouth-watering, died-and-gone-to-heaven taste of meat and potatoes.

He was digging in for more when Marilyn returned, her damp blond hair brushed out and wearing a baggy sweatshirt, blue jeans, and thick socks. She looked much softer now, much more approachable.

"So, where are you off to after you leave Paineville, Mr. Haywood?"

Cross off approachable. This woman was more than ready to pack his bags herself, then personally see him off.

"Marilyn, I didn't raise you to be rude."

"Sorry, Gran. I just think it would be better right off if Mr. Haywood—"

"Dusty."

"—Mr. Haywood knew you made a mistake. You don't need a boarder."

"And how would you know? You aren't home long enough for me to fill you in on the ideas I have for my own house."

"It's not like you need the money."

"Money ain't everything, girl."

Dusty started to rise, plate in hand. "Maybe I should take my plate into the kitchen while you two gals discuss this. Without me."

Ruby Sue reached across the short distance between them and pushed him back down, the force in the petite woman's hand catching him off guard. He'd never make the mistake of misjudging this little dynamo again.

"My granddaughter—who is single, I might add—is speaking out of turn. She don't know what she needs."

"Gran!"

Dusty watched the young woman's face turn a becoming shade of crimson. When she met his eyes with hers, he smiled in commiseration. "I have a grandmother, too."

Marilyn glared at him, obviously not accepting his sympathy. He decided to keep his mouth shut.

Ruby Sue stood, her hands balled at her waist. "You can speak your mind, Marilyn, and so can I. This is still my house and I have the final say on what goes on here."

Marilyn also stood, meeting her grandmother's ire head-on. "Gran, don't do this."

The two women stood in silent stand-off, hitching Dusty's curiosity to full-blown. "Do what?"

The women scowled at each other. Marilyn answered without looking his way.

"She's playing matchmaker."

Dusty choked on a mouthful of green beans.

Ruby Sue turned on her heel and stomped from the room.

Marilyn slowly lowered herself into her seat.

Once he swallowed his food, Dusty found his voice. "Did you say matchmaker?"

Marilyn stared down at her plate. Silence reigned until the clang of pots sounded from the kitchen. She sighed. "Gran's been trying to marry me off for some time now. It's like a holy mission for her. Problem is, she hasn't succeeded."

So matchmaking was why the older woman wanted

to know his age, marital status, if he held a steady job, for the sole purpose of having a responsible boarder. It also explained the big smile when Ruby Sue met him and welcomed him with open arms. Forgetting to ask about references. And going on how a single man like him had found just the right place to settle himself.

"It could be worse," Marilyn informed him, humor infusing her tone. "She could have had the minister waiting in the parlor when you got home from work one day."

Dusty swallowed hard. Just what had he gotten himself into?

The barest trace of a smile tugged at Marilyn's lips. "I'm not joking, I've lived with this woman all my life. It just might happen."

Dusty reached up to scratch his neck. "I just need a place to hang out for a while. No drama, just quiet." He glanced in Marilyn's direction. "I'm not gonna get any quiet, am I?"

This time her smile actually shined in her eyes. "No."

Dusty leaned back and rested his head against the high-back chair. He expelled a long breath. "She got first and last."

"You won't be seeing that money again."

Funny, he expected he'd be angry over all this, but instead he enjoyed the banter. Found his buried sense of humor surfacing. That strange sensation hadn't visited him since . . . well, before he went into business full-time. And wasn't that why he was here, to feel a connection to life again? To people? To wake up the talent that went dormant the minute he stopped doing what he loved to do and started running things?

He glanced at Marilyn again. She suddenly looked dejected and immensely tired, her shoulders slumping as she rubbed her forehead with slender fingers. He imagined he'd looked the same way before he high-tailed it out of Nashville.

"So I'm stuck here for a while?" Oddly enough, the more he thought about it, the more he liked the idea.

"Look, I'm sorry," she said, her voice flat. "I came flying in here like I own the place when Gran is right. It's her house, she can do as she pleases. This whole boarder thing threw me off."

"Hey, it's okay with me. I think it's your grandmother who needs the apology."

"You're right." She dropped her napkin on the table as she rose. "Excuse me."

As Marilyn exited the room, Dusty resumed his meal. Alone. In the quiet.

Like so many times in his life.

Suddenly the realization hit him straight on. He'd rather have those two women in here arguing than face another meal alone.

Marilyn entered the warm kitchen, the heart of this home, and immediately went to embrace her grandmother who stood at the island hooking a pot onto a rack. "I'm sorry," she whispered.

"What's gotten into you, girl?" She hugged back.

"There's something I need to tell you."

Ruby Sue narrowed her eyes.

"I've been offered a job in Charlotte."

The older woman turned and stepped to the sink filled with dishes. "You takin' it?"

Marilyn moved beside her, grabbing a dish towel to help. "I'm thinking about it."

"When?"

"They want an answer by the end of the month."

Ruby Sue, her mouth set, kept scrubbing the pots. "Well, then, we got work to do. The Harvest Festival is weekend after next. And then there's Thanksgiving right after that. You promised to help me."

"Of course I will." Marilyn dried a strainer, waiting for her sometimes gruff, always loving, grandmother to say more. The festival was important, but Marilyn knew that staying plugged into the community helped Ruby Sue deal with her happiness, as well as her disappointments. She suspected Ruby Sue would take Marilyn's words as a major disappointment. "So . . . how do you feel about me leaving?"

"Do I have a choice?" She dropped a pot into the deep porcelain sink. "I knew this was coming, just hoped you'd decide to stay put. Especially when you moved in with me."

"Ty's always around now. He'll help you out."

"Your brother has a brand new wife who is busy with her craft store. Besides, he's got more important things to do. Like working on that brood of grandkids he and Casey promised me."

Marilyn suppressed the all too often rush of . . . something that engulfed her when anyone mentioned marriage and babies. Better not to go there. She couldn't see that in her future.

"They aren't that busy. They'll both do what ever they can. And besides, I'll only be a few hours away."

"Just not the same."

They resumed the chore in silence. Marilyn really

didn't know how to make her leaving easier for her grandmother. It had never been a secret that Marilyn might move on someday, but Ruby Sue always talked her out of it.

This time seemed different. Maybe it was timing. Or that everything was falling into place. Whatever the case, Marilyn needed to clutch the brass ring while she had a chance. She didn't have a husband or kids looming in her future. She'd never given any guy half a chance to get serious with her. Serious meant commitment, and commitment meant settling down, and she'd never found the right man. And she wouldn't make the same mistakes her mom did. So instead, she concentrated on her job. And now she had a chance at fulfilling her dream to succeed beyond Paineville.

So that meant getting things under control at home before she left.

"So, are you really that set on keeping a boarder?"

"I'd think you'd feel better knowin' someone was around after you left."

"But he's a perfect stranger. You don't know anything about him."

"I know enough." Ruby Sue stopped washing, her hands still beneath the sudsy water.

"And I can't talk you out of it?"

"No. But you can do me a favor before you leave."

Marilyn sighed a breath of relief. "Anything. You name it."

"I want you to get to know Dusty before you leave. That way you won't feel bad leavin' me behind. He won't be a stranger then."

Shock momentarily strangled her words. "Get—get to know him better?"

"You said you'd do anything."

"Yes, but—"

"Tryin' to get out of your word?"

Marilyn clamped her lips together. She was well and truly caught.

"Okay?" Ruby Sue badgered.

"Okay," Marilyn agreed, very reluctantly. "So, what do you know about this guy?"

Ruby Sue's shoulders relaxed. "Dusty's a song-writer from Nashville."

"Really." Who would have thought? "Nashville, huh? What's he write? Country? Jingles? Love songs?"

"You'll have to ask him yourself."

"I will." Although she didn't like the idea. He rubbed her the wrong way. She'd never admit to him that he wasn't entirely at fault for her dip in the puddle. But there was more.

Maybe it was his dark good looks and his easygoing temperament that made her uncomfortable. Not in an out-and-out scary stranger sort of way, more like a male-testosterone-attractive sort of way. He got to her on an elemental level.

Not to mention the fact that he'd made himself right at home here much too fast. He may have charmed Ruby Sue, but he wouldn't get to her. No way. Her dates with men may be few and far between, but she knew to keep wary of this guy. Who just ups and leaves Nashville to come to Paineville, of all places, to become a boarder? She'd find out, especially since Ruby Sue wanted her to get to *know* the man.

A loud knock on the swinging door separating the

dining room and kitchen made Marilyn jump. Mr. Haywood leaned into the doorway.

"You ladies okay?"

Marilyn forced a breezy tone. "Just fine."

Ruby Sue took the towel from Marilyn's hands and ushered her granddaughter back toward the dining room. "C'mon Marilyn. We've left our guest to fend for himself."

"Don't worry, ma'am. I've been taking care of myself for a long time."

"Beside, he's not a guest," Marilyn reminded them both.

"You're right," Ruby Sue muttered, out of Marilyn's earshot as she followed the couple into the dining room. "Before long, I'm hoping he'll be part of the family."

Chapter Three

The next morning Marilyn settled into the driver's seat of her Cadillac, turning the key. Nothing. She tried again, then pounded on the steering wheel. "Why me?" she grumbled, determined to make this car start if it was the last thing she did.

After another ten minutes of futile key-turning and intermittent prayer, she stood outside the vehicle, counting to ten before kicking the tire. Just then, her grandmother and Mr. Haywood walked out of the house and joined her on the driveway.

"Trouble?" Mr. Haywood asked, his eyes sparkling with humor.

She took a deep breath. "It won't start. Again."

"Told you it needed a new battery."

"I thought the old one would last a little longer."

"Just call Hank down at the garage," Ruby Sue advised. "He'll tow it to the shop."

"That's fine, but I need a ride to work now."

Mr. Haywood opened the passenger side of his truck. "Jump in. We're headed to town anyway."

"We? As in you and Gran?"

"Yep. She's got some work lined up and asked me to join her. How could I resist after she cooked up such a terrific breakfast?"

"Always said a way to a man's heart is through his stomach," Ruby Sue professed.

"I didn't know you were looking for a man," Marilyn countered.

"Watch it, girl. You're stepping into deep water here."

Marilyn turned away and cursed the heat creeping up her neck when she heard Mr. Haywood's chuckle.

"How very thoughtful of you to offer a ride, Mr. Haywood—"

"Dusty."

Marilyn bit the inside of her cheek. The man had offered her a ride. The least she could do was call him by his first name. For reasons she definitely didn't want to explore, she felt safer calling him by his formal name.

"Thanks, Dusty. I appreciate this."

He gestured with in a wide sweeping motion. "Your carriage awaits."

Ruby Sue nodded in satisfaction. "Now that's a man who knows how to treat a woman right."

"And you know this because he's giving us a ride?"

"No. You got eyes, girl. Figure it out yourself."

Marilyn groaned. Her grandmother could exasperate the most patient person on earth.

"Ladies?"

Dusty stood by the truck, an expectant grin on his lips.

Marilyn clutched her shoulder-strap briefcase close and stepped forward. Ruby Sue trailed behind.

"You first," Marilyn instructed.

"You know I like sittin' by the window."

Marilyn closed her eyes, mentally counting to ten once again, then hiked up her skirt and hauled herself into the cab. She fished in her purse for the new roll of antacids she'd tossed in this morning, already stressing before the day started. Ruby Sue eased onto the seat beside her, her elbow poking Marilyn. Marilyn nearly choked on the dry, powdery tablets as her grandmother forcefully nudged her closer toward the middle of the bench seat, her motions agile for a woman of her advanced age and small size.

Once Marilyn settled in, Dusty closed the door behind them. As he rounded the front of the truck, Marilyn asked, "So, Gran, how did you con him into taking you to town?"

"It wasn't hard. He needed something to do and I needed a ride. We came to an agreement."

"A regular mutual admiration society," Marilyn grumbled under her breath.

Dusty jumped in, his clean, musky aftershave invading Marilyn's senses. He sat close enough for his body heat to invade her space as she unwillingly found herself pressed against him. And not hating it as she'd expected. He reached out to start the ignition, his arm brushing hers. The everyday, normal action sent shivers up her arm.

Not an ordinary, everyday response for her.

Marilyn tried to scoot away as the truck rumbled

down the driveway, but Ruby Sue kept pushing her to the center. All that moving around caused her trench coat to tangle around her legs and her briefcase dug into her side. She sighed and settled in for a ride she had lost all control over.

Dusty and Ruby Sue chattered away while Marilyn tried to endure his nearness by turning her thoughts to her work schedule. She caught snatches of the conversation and before long gave up worrying about work and listened instead.

"How many pumpkins do you think you need for the stand?" Dusty asked.

"About six dozen. We give 'em away to the children after the harvest festival."

"If you need, I can load them into my truck bed."

"Why Dusty, that's more than kind of you."

Marilyn rolled her eyes. Her grandmother was a born flirt. Talk about wrapping a guy around her finger . . .

Ruby Sue's cry suddenly cut through the cab. "Dusty, stop!"

Dusty slammed on the brakes and forcefully extended his right arm across the briefcase Marilyn clutched to her chest. She expelled a rush of air as his reflexive motion kept her from propelling into the dashboard.

"What's wrong?" he shouted, trying to control the truck.

"Densler's Farm stand is open. I have to ask them for a donation to the festival."

Dusty pulled into the gravel drive and shifted the truck into park while Ruby Sue opened the door and eased out of the cab. Marilyn dared a peek in his direction, her pulse rate barely calming after their abrupt stop. She was used to her grandmother's outbursts, but this man wasn't. Especially not while driving.

Dusty's brows were drawn down, but he didn't seem angry. He met her gaze and her stomach tightened. She assured herself it was frustration from her grandmother's behavior, not the clear blue of Dusty's eyes.

"Sorry about that unexpected stop," she muttered.

"Quit saying you're sorry all the time. You didn't do anything."

"Well, um, I guess you're right."

He rolled the window down and leaned his elbow on the frame. "Looks like you'll be late for work."

"That shouldn't be a problem." She hoped.

Silence filled the cab. Marilyn didn't want to be rude and move a full seat away from him, but his nearness made her heart beat uncomfortably faster than normal. She slipped mere inches away, just enough to give her breathing space.

"So, what's a music writer doing in our little Georgia town?"

Dusty stared out the window, no doubt looking at the beautiful landscape created for nature's canvas. The mist was only now burning off the pasture under the bright morning sun. A glimpse of dark mountains could be seen through the wisps of rising fog. Leaves in varying hues of rust, mahogany, and gold created a frame around the picture painted before them.

"Hoping to find my muse," he said in a subdued tone.

"I didn't know you could lose something like that."

He smiled, but the smile didn't reach his eyes when he glanced at her. "Oh, yeah. It happens."

"So how does one, er, find the muse again?"

"That's what I'm hoping to find on this journey."

He didn't seem inclined to elaborate, so Marilyn decided to venture onto different territory. "So, what kind of music do you write?"

"Mostly I write country tunes, anything from ballads to rowdy, foot-stompin' songs. I've written some pop and a couple of love songs."

"Would I know the songs you've written?"

Dusty named off a half dozen major hits by various country artists.

Her jaw dropped. "You wrote those?"

"Every one."

"Really."

He chuckled. "It's not rocket science, although it does take a whole lot of sitting and thinking."

"Maybe so, but I can't hold a tune, let alone try to string words together for a song."

"I know it's a gift, trust me, I don't take it for granted. There've been times in the past when I needed a break, but this time it's different." He shook his head. "This sounds odd, but I can't find the words to explain my predicament. I have all the things people think make you successful: money, a great job, access to famous people. But without the creative gift deep within me, I don't feel all together."

"Because your muse is missing?"

He smiled. "Yeah. In a nutshell."

Marilyn heard her grandmother's voice along with others outside the truck. But nothing seemed as real as sitting here with this man. Getting to know Dusty, just like her grandmother asked. And discovering that this wasn't the horrible experience she'd convinced herself it would be.

"How did you pick Paineville to start your search?"

"I didn't. It picked me."

"Come again?"

He grinned. "I needed a change of scenery, you know, to get away from the rat race. My grandmother, also a meddler, suggested I head down here. She mentioned a few towns where some of our family have lived, so I dropped by Paineville first."

His face softened as he spoke. "It was the weirdest thing. I pulled into town, looking for a place to get a cup of coffee. As I drove, I couldn't help but admire the Victorian storefronts in the town square. I parked in front of a crafts store and watched the shoppers stroll from there to the general store and on to another. A kid's clothing store, I think. Anyway, it just sorta drew me in. No hustle and bustle, just a sleepy little town. Then I went into the café and the smell of coffee and cinnamon buns dragged me in deeper. I eavesdropped on the locals and knew that this was the place where I could spend some time."

"How'd you find out about Ruby Sue?"

"I asked around. I figured that hanging out in this town would provide a wealth of material to get writing again. And if you want color, you hang out with locals." He grinned as he looked over at her. "Apparently you're the only one she didn't tell about this boarder business."

Marilyn shook her head. "She never ceases to amaze me."

Dusty chuckled. "And exasperate."

"That's true."

"Hey, seems like the lady knows what she wants and how to get it."

Marilyn looked out at Densler's field, her job dilemma suddenly weighing on her mind. "She's not the only one."

"Runs in the family?"

"We're all pretty . . . determined."

"Good, maybe some of that attitude will rub off on me." Dusty smiled at her, a genuine smile. A smile that finally reached his perceptive eyes. That sharpened his features. That sent her pulse racing.

She decided since he was approachable, she'd satisfy this curiosity she had about him. "So how do you intend on finding your muse?"

Dusty's expression grew troubled as he turned away, his hands gripping the steering wheel.

"I don't mean to be nosy, but you'd better get used to it if you plan on spending time in Paineville." When he remained silent, she continued. "Nothing goes unnoticed in this town. And everything is open to gossip. Just ask my brother, he's had his share of it and lived to tell the tale."

A ghost of a smile flitted over Dusty's lips.

Marilyn forged on. "I would think that if you've been a songwriter for any length of time, things would just come naturally."

"I can tell you're more of a practical, let's-get-it-done-now type of gal."

A funny hitch tugged at her heart. "I guess I am."

"And you never have times of doubt?"

If only he could read her mind. Doubt plagued her

daily, especially now with the job offer. Instead, she said, "We all have doubts from time to time."

"To a creative mind, any question of your ability can keep you blocked. I fell into the business end of music, away from my true calling. Stuff happened, I reacted, and now the words won't flow. I figured some down time would get me back on track."

Marilyn shifted in her seat. She didn't relate to what he was saying, but her heart went out to him just the same. After all, why would someone come to Paineville on purpose? She barely knew the guy, yet he had touched her with his story.

This had to stop. He was a temporary boarder. She had her sights set on Charlotte. Her grandmother had nefarious plans towards matchmaking. What a convoluted stew she'd been stirred into.

She glanced at her watch, noting the time. Her boss would worry if she didn't show up soon. She was never late.

"Gran," she called out. "If you don't hurry I'm going to have to walk to work."

Ruby Sue waved. "Gimme a minute, girl."

Marilyn slumped against the seat. "Her minute could take an hour."

"Want me to leave her, run you to town, and come back?"

Oh, wouldn't Ruby Sue just love that. "No. I'll give her five more minutes."

Dusty's thumb bounced on the steering wheel while Marilyn pulled her skirt more comfortably around her.

"Do you play an instrument?" she asked.

"Piano and guitar."

"Multi-talented. I'm impressed." She warmed up to

this information-gathering. "Did you see the piano in our living room?"

"Hard to miss it."

"Maybe you'll be able to sit down and come up with some ideas. Usually it's quiet around the house. And Gran would enjoy hearing—"

"I'll think about it."

"Oh. Right. You have to find your muse first."

He shifted in his seat. "Since we're being so chatty here, want to tell me what that arguing at the dinner table was all about last night? Aside from the match-making issue."

Marilyn stared out the window, her back rigid, not ready to let her personal defenses down. After all, the conversation had been on safe ground when discussing him. "Nothing really. Not worth talking about."

"That didn't sound like nothing to me. Hey, it's only fair you share some here. I told you about my dilemma, and trust me, it doesn't get any more personal than that."

He was right. He deserved more than her silence. "I've been offered a job in Charlotte. Gran doesn't want me to move, but I want to get out of this town."

"Why?"

Why, indeed. Probably because of the memories etched in her heart. Memories of whispers and giggles in Sunday school class when the other girls stayed away from Marilyn. Memories of her mother coming home late almost every night, along with the angry phone calls or stares when the family walked down Main Street. That treatment had long ago stopped, but the lasting impressions refused to leave Marilyn's psyche.

She brushed off his question with her usual vague answers. "Ancient history. Besides, I want to see if I can be successful somewhere other than my home town."

"Everyone should strike out on their own to prove themselves." Dusty twisted in the seat to face her. "I don't know your history but can I offer a word of advice?"

"Sure. Why not? Everyone else does."

He chuckled before turning serious again. "Make sure it's really what you want. Getting where you think you want to be isn't as rewarding as getting to where you definitely should be."

"Sounds mystic."

"Not really. Life experience. The best, and hardest, teacher there is."

She nodded. "Okay. I'll think about it."

"And if you need someone to talk to, someone who isn't family and therefore biased, look me up. I'm in the bedroom at the other end of the hallway."

Marilyn caught her breath. His reminder of their close proximity at home made her stomach dance. She wondered why she took antacids when they never seemed to work.

Dusty grinned, causing Marilyn's heart to accelerate again. His blue eyes, with small lines fanning from the corners, captured her attention. Suddenly she forgot why she was sitting in this truck, forgot all about work, and for long seconds, almost forgot her name.

All because her grandmother's boarder smiled at her and the sun seemed to shine brighter.

Uh-oh. She swallowed.

Dusty Haywood was trouble.

Chapter Four

Later that day, Dusty pulled the truck into a parking space a few doors away from the real estate office. Marilyn wouldn't be too pleased that he'd been recruited to bring her home, so he let the truck idle a minute before making his entrance.

He thought about Ruby Sue's blatant suggestion that he pick up Marilyn. Actually, he'd been trying to decide if he should offer, so Ruby Sue's timing proved perfect. Thoughts of Marilyn had captivated him more than once today, and he found himself wanting to spend time alone with her, even though she'd made it clear she wished he'd head back to Tennessee. That wasn't going to happen any time soon. He had no desire to return to the debacle of his recently ended record-producing career.

It started when he lost a contract with a talented young artist named Johnnie Kay. The guy had a strong voice and unique style. At the executives' urging, Dusty strong-armed him into changing his sound once they got into the studio. The execs wanted Johnnie to sound like a carbon copy of one of their already famous artists. They could see dollar signs. And since they were footing the bill, Dusty went along with their request.

Johnnie, not happy about the change, quit. The company was not pleased by the desertion and hassle over the contract. Dusty's partner, who handled the business dealings, dropped the ball. Right into Dusty's lap. But Dusty recovered quickly, finding another act to redeem his image.

Was it only a month ago that he'd been in the studio, ready to cut a record? Leather and Lace, a local Nashville band, had demonstrated raw talent. He'd offered them a deal and they'd jumped at the chance, promising to do whatever it took to make their music happen. But as soon as they went into the studio, good intentions quickly deteriorated.

The band members bickered among themselves and quickly lost focus. Dusty spent more time as a den father than producer. The record company caught wind of the costly chaos and threatened to pull out if Dusty couldn't deliver a quality recording. The final straw came when the lead singer, a voluptuous redhead, announced her undying love for Dusty. She wanted to quit the band and marry him.

From there, the deal went south. As he was the producer, all blame fell at Dusty's feet. His partner denied any blame, telling the record label he didn't know about any problems. Disgusted, Dusty cut his losses, told the band it was over, and callously informed the barely-out-of-her-teens singer there would be no marriage.

Words about Dusty, like "heartless" and "cutthroat", were bandied around, but fell on deaf ears. Dusty went home, packed his bag, and headed south, never looking back.

And hadn't written a song since.

He stared out the truck window at the cars passing through the square. How many folks were headed home to family or out on the town? Life went on, even as his hovered in limbo.

So here he sat, stranded in uncertainty. The long hours and countless lives he manipulated in the name of music came back to haunt him. That part of his life was over and he planned to move on. To start over.

Until he realized his gift for songwriting had vanished. Literally ceased to exist. And for that loss, he grieved deeply.

With a disgusted sigh, he switched off the ignition and stepped down from the truck. His boots thudded on asphalt, his steps slow as he approached the real estate office. He wasn't in a hurry to come in from the cold. At least the chill penetrated his senses and he felt . . . *something*.

Lights from the storefronts flickered in the twilight as the autumn shadows of dusk coalesced around him. He jerked the collar of his lined denim jacket higher and ducked into Marilyn's office, surprised at his heightened anticipation of seeing her. Deep down, he hoped Marilyn would calm down about this boarder business. At least long enough so he could get to know her before she decided to pack up for Charlotte.

She looked up as he entered, surprise flickering in her cocoa-colored eyes. "What're you doing here?"

"Ruby Sue sent me to pick you up."

"What about my car?"

"With all the running around we did today, she forgot to call the garage before it closed."

Marilyn straightened the papers on her desk and frowned. "You know what she's doing, don't you? She didn't call the garage on purpose."

He shrugged, enjoying her pique. "I'll take care of it tomorrow. But in the meantime, you need a ride home."

She paused for a moment, then reached down behind her desk. "Just let me get my belongings and we can go. Everyone else has gone home, so I have to lock up."

"Take your time."

He watched her hustle around the office, her shapely legs not quite hidden by the long coat she'd worn this morning. Her navy suit, one that screamed professionalism, failed to conceal the attractive woman inside. Normally Dusty didn't go for the driven type, but when Marilyn let her guard down and softened in that feminine way, he found himself spellbound. She might have her make-up applied to perfection and her blond hair styled to today's fashion, but when that look of uncertainty lingered her eyes, he was captivated. It surprised him that Marilyn was the only woman he'd ever considered taking home to live happily ever after with.

Even though he didn't have a home to take her to.

He glanced at his watch. "Do you always work this late?"

"Usually."

"It's dinnertime."

She shrugged as she grabbed a file folder and

slipped it into her briefcase. "Sometimes I lose track of time."

He grinned. "I can relate. It's like that when I write."

Marilyn jerked her keen gaze to his. They stared in silence for long static seconds while he waited for her comment.

When she didn't speak, he shoved his hands in his jeans pockets. "Listen, your grandmother has an errand for us before we go home."

Her eyes narrowed. "What kind of errand? The way you two came in and out of town today, I thought you'd be finished."

"You noticed?"

"Noticed what?"

"That I came in and out of town today?"

Marilyn dropped her gaze as she busied with straightening her desk. "I couldn't help but notice. My grandmother makes a scene just about everywhere she goes."

He chuckled, enjoying the way she tried to hide her flustered face from his. So she had noticed him today? Her jerky movements confirmed her discomfort. She draped her purse strap over her shoulder and passed by him, heading to the front door.

Dusty followed. "That she does, but she knows how to get a job done, especially with the Harvest Festival coming up. Everyone listens and does whatever she asks. I've seen record execs who couldn't get as much done in one day as she in an hour."

"Then why another errand?"

"You know, so she can keep throwing us together."

Marilyn laughed as she brushed the light switch

with her elegantly polished rose-colored fingernails. "Are you sure this doesn't bother you? Ruby Sue's antics?"

"Nope. Bother you?"

"I can put up with it if you can," she replied, her tone a challenge as she locked the door.

They stepped out to the sidewalk. "Anyway," Dusty continued, "Ruby Sue wants us to stop at some place called The Saucy Sow. There's a local bluegrass band playing and she wants my opinion on hiring them as entertainment for the festival."

"She wants us to do that tonight?"

"Apparently this is next on her to-do list. She panicked because she couldn't see them tonight, since she had something planned. She knows I have experience in music, so I told her we'd do the job."

Marilyn stopped and held up her hand. "Wait, my grandmother never panics."

"Well, it seemed that way to me."

"You could have gone before you picked me up."

"The band doesn't play till eight o'clock, so I figured we could grab a bite to eat first."

"This isn't asking too much?"

"Hey, it falls in my area of expertise. I'm glad to help your grandmother out. I just have one problem."

"And what's that?"

"I don't know the area, not even a good place for dinner, so I need a guide to get me around."

"Anyone would be happy to give you directions."

"Maybe. But I'd only be happy if that someone was you."

She glanced at him, her eyes wide with surprise. She blinked a few times and pushed her hair behind her ear. Holding back a chuckle, he decided he really, really liked it when she let down her guard and just let herself be.

They reached the truck and Dusty unlocked the door. "C'mon. It'll be fun. And you can tell Ruby Sue you helped me out. She'd like that."

"Fine." She stiffly hauled herself into the cab. "Let's get going."

Dusty jogged to his side and slid into the cab. "Where do you want to eat?"

As he put the truck in gear, Marilyn pointed west. "Go around the square and down the hill. The Saucy Sow should do."

"That's where the band is playing."

She turned a forced smile on him and nodded. "Exactly. We can eat, listen, and go right home."

He chuckled out loud. She wasn't going to make this easy on him.

They pulled up to a squat wooden building where heavy plumes of smoke billowed from a chimney around the back. She led him up sagging steps to a creaky door leading to an open room with scattered wooden tables and a stage setup in the far corner. Dusty's stomach rumbled at the smokey wood scent mixed with tangy barbeque.

As he held open the door, four women exited, laughing and talking amongst themselves. In the dim lighting, Dusty noticed Marilyn's mouth draw into a grim line. Her eyes narrowed as she avoided the women. This couldn't be good.

"Marilyn." A tall woman, obviously the leader of the pack, stopped in greeting.

"Kitty."

Kitty looked at Dusty, her eyes wide. "And who have we here?"

"A friend. Dusty Haywood, this is Kitty Leacock. And associates."

"Pleased to meet you." Kitty held out her hand adorned with multiple rings and fairly purred with delight.

Dusty took hers in a quick shake before dropping her hand and edging closer to Marilyn.

"Are you here for business or pleasure?" Although she was addressing Marilyn, Kitty never once took her eyes from Dusty.

"Yes." Marilyn supplied the answer. "And we have to go. See you later."

She dug her fingers into Dusty's sleeve and pulled him into the building, leaving a sputtering Kitty behind.

"Want to explain that?"

"My arch nemesis. She's single. You owe me."

He laughed. "That's good enough for me."

"Just keep your eyes out for her when you're in town. Her claws sink pretty deep."

"I'll be sure to wear my armor."

Marilyn headed straight to an open counter. Beside the opening, a large menu covered the wall, listing pork barbeque, sandwiches, beans and coleslaw, along with desserts and drinks.

"Low overhead here," he commented.

"Wait till you taste the food." Marilyn grinned at him as he ordered. They found a table away from the groups of families and regulars.

"Let me guess, this place is a town institution."

"This was the first restaurant established in the area. It's been owned by the same family for generations."

A waitress brought their drinks.

Dusty lifted his in a toast. "To our working together. May your grandmother be pleased with the results. Of the errand, that is."

Marilyn nodded and laughed, her voice low and heady. "Here, here."

Minutes later the waitress arrived with the food. Dusty's eyes widened at the mound of barbeque and fixins heaped on each plate.

"Dig in," Marilyn encouraged.

He didn't need much encouragement. Not when he derived pleasure in the sight of this highbrow businesswoman sinking her teeth into a meaty rib. He'd died and gone to pork heaven.

By the time they'd finished, the band came in, setting up their instruments. "So, how are these guys?" Dusty asked between mouthfuls of food.

"Pretty good, at least by Paineville standards. I know they've played at state and local fairs. I hear they're serious about going professional."

Dusty decided not to comment on that. How many times had he heard about so-called professional bands, only to check them out and find that they should stay local? The proof would be in their musical talent.

Shortly after eight, the lights dimmed and the band, Dixie Highway, launched into a foot-stompin' number that set the entire place jumping. Dusty pulled his chair around the table so he could watch the group dynamic, as well as sit closer to Marilyn. She didn't nudge away, as he'd half expected. Like everyone else in the place, she was caught up in the music.

Twenty numbers later, the lead singer announced a break. The house lights brightened. Marilyn pinned him with her gaze.

"So?" she asked, a slight hint of challenge in her voice.

"Okay. They're good."

She shook her head. "Try again."

"Okay. Better than good. Just like the food. Just like this town."

She straightened, a satisfied smile pulling her lips. "Thanks. Besides, my cousin is playing the banjo up there. I'm partial to them."

Dusty laughed. "Now I know I've been set up."

Marilyn beamed. "By the best."

When the band returned for their second set, the pace slowed to ballads and love songs. Marilyn swayed, her shoulder brushing his. Startled, she stilled and stared at him out of the corner of her eye. He searched her expression for any hint of attraction, as he always did when she let her guard down and her features softened. He read the sweet invitation of her lips, aware that she didn't consciously realize the message she was sending him. He leaned closer, wanting to kiss her. She didn't move.

The song ended, claps and hoots invading their private moment as the lights came up. Marilyn pulled back, her eyes narrowed with wariness.

"I think we've heard enough." Marilyn slowly stood, easing her arms into her coat sleeves before he had a chance to help her.

He threw a tip on the table and followed her out, dismayed by the rigid set of her shoulders. Gone was the woman who'd briefly allowed him to see her soft side. The all-business woman had returned.

"I'm not going anywhere with Dusty again." Marilyn pushed away her barely-eaten breakfast and bunched her fists beneath the kitchen table. Dusty's potent charm left her feeling off-center, and she was pretty sure he'd wanted to kiss her last night. Problem was, she wanted him to. Wondered all night what it would feel like, taste like.

But then she thought about moving to Charlotte, and she knew she couldn't get involved with him.

"Yes, you will go with him." Ruby Sue stood arms akimbo, her eyes narrowed.

"Didn't you hear me? I said no. It's my first Saturday off in months and I have an hair appointment—"

"You have to go," Ruby Sue interrupted. "I told Buddy Lee you'd be at the stables this afternoon. I know he's got the best animals around, and he's more than happy to let us use them at the festival. But you've been riding and you can judge which ponies will be gentle with the children ridin' on them."

"Let Dusty go by himself." She gestured out the window to where Dusty leaned against his truck. Waiting. "He seems to like being at your beck and call."

"He's polite, unlike some people I know. And you know he doesn't know his way around these parts just yet."

"Still—"

"Still, nothin'. I need you to do this, Marilyn. This festival means a lot to me." For a few seconds the older woman grew quiet, an uncharacteristic vulnerability softening her eyes. Marilyn's resolve wavered.

"And besides, Arlette called a few minutes ago. She had to cancel your hair appointment."

Wonderful. Now she'd have to go around with dark roots until she could get back to the salon. "Gran, I don't want to go."

"And I'm askin' you to help. It's not like you're gonna be around that much longer." She laid a petite hand over her heart.

Marilyn closed her eyes and pinched the bridge of her nose. Guilt. What a lousy motivator. "Fine. I'll do it."

Ruby Sue relaxed. "You're a good girl."

If only I wasn't, Marilyn breathed to herself. Why couldn't she be selfish, like her mother had been, and take off on a whim? Or have the strength to say no to her grandmother's wiles, like her brother, Ty, did? No, she had to be a good girl. The dependable one.

When their mother left, Gran never let on how she felt. She was too busy raising Marilyn and her brothers. Later, when Gabe left, it was different. He'd gotten married and had a great job offer. Gran had come to terms with it. But they'd all missed Ty when he eventually left to pursue a career in construction after a broken engagement. For the first time, Gran let it be known just how much she missed her brood. She and Ty had a special bond, one that Marilyn didn't understand, but respected. She loved them both and knew they loved her in return.

So with her brothers gone, Marilyn had stayed behind, telling herself it would only be for a little while. In the meantime, she changed her shy, backwards image and went totally high maintenance. Ironically, she'd used Kitty as her model. And it worked, she had gotten into real estate with a good measure of success.

Now Ty was home, having finally overcome the tough circumstances that had kept him away, and Gabe would be here to visit soon. Wasn't it her time to strike out on her own? Her time to shine?

She trudged upstairs to change into jeans and an oatmeal cable knit sweater. On the way out, she pulled her hair into a ponytail, and positioned a battered NASCAR cap on her head. Her old hiking boots, worn comfortable through the years, clumped loudly as she crossed the wood porch to meet Dusty at his truck.

He pushed away from the vehicle to meet her. "Ready to go horseback riding?"

"Riding? I thought we were only supposed to check out the ponies for the festival."

"That's what Ruby Sue wants. I haven't been riding in years, so I thought maybe we could go out for a while."

"Why not?" she muttered under her breath. "It's not like I had anything important, like a hair appointment, today."

"I heard that." Dusty flashed her a smile before leaping up into the cab. Marilyn followed suit.

After a quick run-down in directions, Dusty drove out to the Half Moon Stables. He followed the main road until he reached the turnoff Marilyn pointed out. From there, the paved road quickly dissolved into dirt and gravel. The rutted roadway meandered for about a mile through trees bright with autumn foliage. Marilyn had to admit, the bright blue sky and crisp temperature did lend to a play day, something she hadn't indulged in for a long time.

"Don't look at this as family duty," Dusty counseled. "Think of it as a day to relax and smell the roses. Or horses, in this case."

"I have a hard time relaxing."

"So did I. But I learned to slow down. Best thing that ever happened to me."

A short wooden bridge suspended the truck from a bustling creek that led to Half Moon Falls. With the windows down, Marilyn heard the rush of water tumbling over the rocky creek bed.

"Have you started writing?" Marilyn ventured to ask.

His smile waned a bit. "No. I suppose it'll take a while. For now, I'm just taking one day at a time."

"Turn up ahead."

Dusty turned into a smooth area of packed dirt wide enough for vehicles to park. A man strolled out of the nearby stables to greet them.

"Hey, Marilyn. Ruby Sue said you'd be by."

"Hey, Buddy Lee. You know how she is when she's in charge." Marilyn slammed the truck door and walked toward a tall, stocky man about her age. He wore a T-shirt under overalls that had seen better days. Holes pocked the shirt and dirt streaked over the denim. "I know you've got the best ponies around, but she wants me to see them up close and personal."

Buddy Lee chuckled, his pale eyes viewing Marilyn like a man who'd gone too long without food. "Fine with me. Been a long time since I've seen you."

Marilyn lifted her hands in defense. "Work."

"You should slow down."

"So I've heard."

Buddy Lee's eyes narrowed as Dusty came to stand beside her. "Who's your friend?"

"Oh, this is Dusty. He's a . . . sort of . . . friend of Ruby Sue's."

Dusty reached out to shake the other man's hand. "Actually, I'm boarding with Mrs. Callahan."

Buddy Lee scratched his shaggy head. "Heard she'd got some idea to take in boarders. You just never know with Ruby Sue. I've known her all my life, and she still up and does things that surprise us all."

"Why don't we check out the animals?" Marilyn suggested.

"And then go riding," Dusty added. "I called earlier and made a reservation."

"Right. Got two horses lined up for you."

Marilyn fell into step beside Dusty as Buddy Lee led the way.

"You had a hard time admitting I was a boarder at Ruby Sue's. Still have a problem with it?"

"It's not so much you as the situation."

Dusty grinned. "Thanks."

"You're welcome."

"What's so bad about this situation?"

"My family has always been considered odd, I guess. Ruby Sue raised my brothers and me, but we kids always felt like outsiders. I guess when Gran does something out of the ordinary, like taking in a boarder, folks take it in stride, like they expect her to do the unexpected. I suppose it's always made me uncomfortable. Our family reputation has always been a bit . . . tarnished."

Banners never amounted to much and never will.

She'd worked hard to prove those words wrong, but the memories still lingered. She'd spent long hours working to become successful, so it wasn't that she was afraid to abandon the family like her parents had. It was more that she wanted the people she respected, the people she saw day to day, to see that the Banners did amount to something.

"So now you follow the straight and narrow?" Dusty surmised. "Don't deviate from what you consider the road to success?"

She glanced at him, the surprise of his understanding causing a hitch in the area of her heart. "Something like that."

He nodded. "Sometimes the road isn't as straight as you think it is."

"But I want it to be."

Dusty sighed. "And there's the problem."

They stopped at the fence connected to the side of the barn. Inside a large pen four ponies playfully trotted about. Dusty hooked the heel of his Tony Lama boots on the lower crossbar of the fence and rested his forearms on the top rail as he watched the animals.

"Boy, to be that free . . ."

Marilyn leaned against the fence beside him. "What's wrong, Mr. Advice? You sound envious."

"A little."

"Care to elaborate?"

"Maybe later."

"Oh, it's okay to badger—"

"So, what do you think?" Buddy Lee asked as he approached, effectively cutting off the beginning of Marilyn's banter.

"Buddy Lee, they're beautiful. Sweet temperaments,

too. We really appreciate you donating the rides for the festival."

"No problem. Besides, if your grandmother hadn't asked, my mama would have done it anyway. We like to help out."

They stood, admiring the scene, when Buddy Lee announced that he would go get the horses ready for their ride. "You two wait here, I'll be back in a minute."

Marilyn turned and rested her back against the fence to stare into the dense wood, her mind replaying childhood memories. "I used to come here all the time when I was a kid. I loved to ride. To get away from my troubles. Of course, I had to clean stalls in exchange, but I think it was an even deal."

All her life she'd wanted to be normal: a family with both parents at home, a regular house like all her friends. Instead, each parent took off and she'd grown up in a run-down trailer.

Her father had disappeared and her mother hadn't stayed in one place very long. Occasionally her mother would call to give a new address or phone number. Then she finally married a man, but never asked her children to come meet her new husband.

Marilyn knew that was why she worked so hard to succeed, to make a decent name for herself. And that only something life-altering, like being struck by a lightning bolt, would keep her from attaining her goal.

Dusty's calm voice cut into her thoughts. "And now? Don't you like to ride anymore?"

"Now I don't have time."

Buddy Lee had the horses saddled and ready to go. She watched as Dusty stepped into the stirrups and swung a muscled, denim-clad leg over the horse. Leather creaked as he settled into the saddle.

The mare danced, agitated by the new rider. Dusty grabbed hold of the reins, pulling while he clicked his tongue and spoke gently, strong fingers caressing the animal's sleek neck with the skill of a patient lover. Soothing words failed to hide the command in his tone, and yet the horse complied and settled down.

Marilyn swallowed as she viewed his sinewy legs controlling the horse, the way the muscles in his arms worked as he adjusted the reins. "Done this before?" she asked as she grabbed the horn to pull herself up.

"Yeah. A friend of mine lived on a farm. We used to ride."

Buddy Lee adjusted the bridle of Marilyn's horse one last time. "Remember to stay on the trail. It's changed some since you last went out. The horses know, but I don't want you wandering off."

"Got it. We'll be careful."

She shifted in the saddle, squeezing her legs to nudge the horse in a slow trot. Before long they were traveling deep into the woods. Other than the clop of hooves on the packed dirt, Marilyn enjoyed the silence.

Buddy Lee was right, it had been a while since she'd ridden. She closed her mind from the cares and drama in her life and drank in the beauty of the fall day. Multi-colored leaves made a canopy overhead. Every once in a while she reached out to capture one of the leaf-laden twigs. The scents of leather and horse mingled together to arouse hidden memories in her mind. Yes, she had missed these quiet rides. The simpler times of life when decisions weren't life-altering and responsibilities weren't so important.

She glanced over her shoulder at Dusty. His tanned hands held the reins loosely and his relaxed posture proved he was more than comfortable on a horse.

Although grateful for the quiet solitude Dusty had afforded her, the time came to make polite conversation.

"So, what else has my grandmother roped you into?" she asked, breaking the silence.

Dusty chuckled. "Let's see. Tomorrow she's got us going to church. Then a big family dinner with your brother, Ty, and his wife. Then, on Monday, we have to visit some of her friends to pass out job assignments."

"I can't believe you know more about what's going on than I do."

Dusty ducked under a low-hanging branch. "I'm having a good time."

"Being manipulated? She's good at that, you know."

A shadow passed over Dusty's eyes. "She doesn't even rate."

"And how would you know?"

"It takes one to know one, and I was the best."

Marilyn slowed her horse so Dusty could come up beside her. "You? Scheming and manipulative? I find that hard to believe."

"I'm not proud of it, but there it is."

"I thought you wrote music. Isn't that a pretty solitary job?"

"When I'm writing, yes. But until recently, I produced records."

"And . . . ?"

"Do you know what a producer does?"

"Produce?" Marilyn nudged her horse to move.

"Funny." Dusty flicked the reins so his horse followed suit. "Basically we work in the studio with the musicians. With state-of-the-art equipment, we make a certain sound or style to the music."

"That doesn't sound manipulative."

"Ah, but it is. We control how the music sounds, what type of image will come from the recordings. To do that, I have to convince the artists to do things in a certain way, whether they like it or not."

"I see. So you're saying that you did this to people . . . artists . . . and you didn't like it?"

"No. Neither did they."

"Then why keep at it? Why not just write music?"

"Things got complicated. I have a knack for hearing the right sounds, making things flow. And I'm good at it." He patted the horse's neck. "A friend asked me to help him, we became partners, and the next thing I knew, I got deeper into the complex aspects of recording music. I made more money than some of the artists. Pretty soon my reputation as the best producer in town went to my head. I went into the partnership with the sole intention of managing the creative side of things. My partner fell short on his promises and the next thing I knew, the business side took over. Eventually, the writing took a distant second place."

A small slope fanned out before them, leading to the edge of a sparkling lake.

"You must regret that now."

"I do." Dusty's turbulent gaze met hers. It looked as though she'd stumbled onto Dusty's sore spot. He always seemed to know what buttons to push with her; now she'd finally found his.

"Let's sit by the lake," he said.

Marilyn gazed at the calm water, a smile pulling her lips. Maybe he needed someone to listen. "For a few minutes."

They dismounted, securing the reins to the nearby branches of a tree. Marilyn sat on a boulder warmed by the afternoon sun, near the water's edge. Dusty cocked his hip against the large rock, his shoulder brushing hers. With any other man she'd have inched away. But not with Dusty. Even though tremors skittered down her arm, she felt safe with him as she did with no other person. And again, she wondered why.

After a few quiet minutes, Dusty broke the silence. "I don't know why you and your grandmother go round and round. I figure that's your concern. But I've spent enough time with Ruby Sue the last few days to know that your leaving is pretty hard on her."

She opened her mouth to speak but he held up his hand. "I'm not saying that to make you change your mind. I have a feeling your grandmother won't let you know how she really feels."

Her shoulders slumped. "You're right about that."

"And I suspect you don't come out and tell her what's going on with you."

"Guilty as charged."

He took her hand and entwined it in his. "Don't let your job become your life, Marilyn. I've seen too many good people become consumed until they're nothing but an empty shell. You're too beautiful, have too much in life in you, to settle for that."

Dusty leaned over and gently brushed his lips over

hers. The moment—so perfect, so dreamlike—lulled Marilyn into responding. She hesitated at first, remembering her earlier vow of not getting involved. But when Dusty deepened the kiss, she leaned into him, willingly participating, not wanting the moment to end. For once she didn't fight her emotions. This man seemed to know her so well, know her secret wants and desires. In her heart she wanted this more than she'd ever admit.

He broke this kiss, his firm fingers stroking her hair. He smiled, not caring where she came from, or who her mother had been.

"Think about what I said," he whispered, taking her lips again. She sighed and sank into him, her free hand wrapping around his neck to finger the hair at his collar.

One of the horses snorted, dragging Marilyn from her dream world. As much as she wanted to linger here with Dusty, a part of her warned that the emotional circumstances might be more than she could handle right now. She had business decisions to make, not personal ones.

"We'd better get back. Buddy Lee gets all worked up if his horses aren't returned in the slotted time."

Dusty nodded, reluctantly stepping back so she could slide off the boulder.

"He has a crush on you, you know."

Her mouth gaped open. "He does not."

"Does too."

"Yeah, well, Kitty has her eyes on you."

Dusty shrugged off her comment, clearly not concerned about the other woman. "I can deal with her. But this guy has it bad for you."

"C'mon, Buddy Lee? I've known him almost my whole life."

"What difference does that make?"

Try as she might, Marilyn just couldn't picture it. "That's crazy."

"What? That a guy could be interested in you?"

She didn't answer, afraid of what she'd say. Afraid to admit that her darkest nightmare was that she might become a joke to everyone in town, like her mother had been. That's why she worked so hard at being an upstanding citizen.

She returned to her horse, eager to get out of here, to end this conversation.

Once they both mounted, Marilyn led them back toward the stable. The late afternoon sun cast long shadows over the leaf-strewn path.

"I don't know who hurt you," Dusty said quietly, "but I sure would like to make it better for you."

She knew he couldn't, so she finished the ride back in silence.

Chapter Five

Marilyn tossed and turned in her bed for hours. Finally, she glared at the alarm clock. Two in the morning? With a groan, she crawled from the covers to head downstairs. She snatched the ragged chenille robe at the foot of her bed and tugged it over her blue T-shirt and plaid flannel baggies.

Maybe getting something to eat would distract her from her scattered thoughts. Not only had Dusty bothered her all day with his constant proximity every time she turned around, but did his handsome image have to intrude on her dreams as well?

Two big chocolate chip cookies later, she felt mildly better. Memories of her life spun round and round in her mind while she agonized over her decision of leaving Paineville. Even at twenty-eight, her mother's abandonment still hurt deeply. Perhaps because it had never resolved itself, leaving a tiny open wound in Marilyn's heart.

How could she leave her own children? Marilyn still

couldn't fathom such a thing. She swore she wouldn't be like her mother, flighty and self-centered. And she'd succeeded in that: by keeping relationships to a minimum and pretending—even to her own family—that she was content with her life.

And she had been content. Or so she'd thought. Until Dusty showed up, knocking down her defenses, giving her advice, melting the ice that had frozen around her heart.

She didn't want to think about the last part. If he managed to sneak in and permeate her life any further, she'd be lost for sure. She had plans, goals. Besides, he didn't seem to know what he wanted out of his own life right now. How could he even think about any type of relationship with her?

And when she moved? That would only complicate matters. She was definitely *not* of the opinion that absence made the heart grow fonder.

The sugar from the cookies only managed to make her more wired and she hadn't solved any problems. Instead, things had become more muddled *with* her meandering thoughts. Breathing a sigh, she cleaned up the crumbs and turned off the kitchen light before trudging back toward the stairs leading to her cold and lonely bedroom.

She shuffled through the dining room, coming to a stop in the foyer. She didn't remember any lights on when she came downstairs. Now, a faint glow chased the shadows in the living room. Unnerved, she quietly grabbed an umbrella from the hall stand and stepped ahead, peeking into the room, her weapon poised.

Dusty sat at the piano, a thick lock of dark hair falling over his furrowed forehead as he stared down at the piano. As if in slow motion, he lifted his hands over the keyboard, trembling fingers suspended in mid-air. He slowly lowered them just short of touching the ivory keys, as if he expected to touch white hot fire.

Marilyn held her breath.

Then, just as slowly, Dusty closed his eyes and raised his hands, bunching them into tight balls. He held the position, not moving.

The sudden need to comfort him overpowered Marilyn. But she respected his privacy. On tiptoe she backed away, replacing the umbrella before climbing the stairs. To her surprise, she didn't release her breath until she safely closed the door to her bedroom.

The ringing telephone blared over the chaos in the Banner kitchen. A homey warmth enveloped the heart of the home. Ruby Sue reached around Marilyn to grab her special spice bottle and sprinkle the mixture into a steaming pot of greens as Marilyn cracked the oven door to check on her browning apple pie, the cinnamon-sweet aroma gently released into the air around them.

"I've got it," Marilyn hollered. She ducked out of her grandmother's way, sidestepped her sister-in-law, Casey, who'd come over to help in the kitchen, and grabbed the receiver from the wall phone. "Hello?"

"Hey, little sister, how are you?"

"Gabe! I'm great. How are you and Emily?"

"We're fine." He paused for a moment. "Just wanted to connect with the family. Figured you'd all be there for Sunday dinner."

"We are. The kitchen is crazy. Now that Casey can

cook, she and Gran try to outdo each other." She smiled at Casey, who spilled the canister of flour onto the counter.

"And Ty's probably in front of the television watching the game."

"Yeah. One look at his wife and grandmother drawing the battle lines, he high-tailed it out of here." The crash of a pan followed by Casey's cry of apology made her flinch. "Ty and Dusty are safe for now."

"Dusty?"

Uh oh. She hesitated. "Gran's boarder."

"Her what?"

She chuckled. "You heard me right."

"Since when?"

"About a week. It's okay, he's not a psycho or anything."

"What was she thinking?"

Marilyn started humming the Wedding March.

Gabe groaned. "Are you okay with this?"

"Do I have a say in the matter? Actually, Dusty's a nice guy and for some reason he doesn't mind Gran's interference. He thinks it's funny. He's got a meddling grandmother of his own."

"You better hold on to this one. Another guy may not take to our family."

"I don't think so." Marilyn balked. "He's here temporarily, and if things go well, I might be moving to Charlotte."

"Charlotte? What's there?"

"A chance to make it on my own," she answered, unsure if she was trying to convince her brother or herself.

"I thought you were already doing that."

"Sure, but in a place I've always lived. I want to strike out and see what kind of stuff I'm made of. Like you and Ty have."

"Marilyn." His voice dropped low. Conviction, as well as a deep sadness, sounded there. "There really isn't any place like home, Sis."

Troubled by Gabe's tone, Marilyn ventured carefully. "So, what's up?"

"I wanted to let Gran know that Emily and I will be home for the Harvest Festival."

"That's great! Gran'll do cartwheels."

"Hold her back. Because there's more."

She waited for his news. Her brother always had enjoyed the dramatic.

"Emily and I are moving back home. I wanted to let Gran know because we need a place to stay for a while."

Marilyn squealed and placed her palm over the mouthpiece. "Gabe's coming home. For good."

Ruby Sue dropped her wooden spoon into the pot of potatoes and marched over. "Gimme that phone. Gabe, what's this I hear?"

Marilyn grinned at Casey who had flour up to her elbows. "Well, it looks like Gran's prayers are answered. All of her family back together."

Casey shot her a knowing look. "For how long?"

Taken back at her sister-in-law's stern tone, Marilyn had to pause. "I haven't given the office a final date. Gran still won't talk about it." She glanced at Casey, uneasiness skittering down her spine. "You didn't tell Ty?"

"No. I promised you I wouldn't." Casey sighed.

"Marilyn, you knew Ruby Sue would be unhappy about your decision to move."

"I hoped maybe she'd be excited. Like I was."

"Was?" Casey raised a brow, eyeing her suspiciously.

"No, I'm still excited. I finally have a chance to find out what I'm made of."

"You know what you're made of. Who do you have to prove yourself to?"

She frowned. Who did she have to prove anything to? The question had haunted her for so long in her life that she didn't know the answer anymore. She just knew she had to go.

Casey cast her a knowing look. "Sounds like something happened to change your mind? Or someone?"

Dusty, a voice whispered inside her.

Marilyn vehemently shook her head. "Gran's mind. I feel bad leaving her. Obviously her decision to take in a boarder was a cry for company." She paused to smile. "Gran doesn't need help. She usually manipulates."

"True, but something must be bothering her. Why else would she let Dusty, a perfect stranger, live here?"

Marilyn picked up a wooden spoon and stirred the green beans. "That woman always has her reasons," she replied and left it at that.

"If you even consider staying, I'll bet the man sitting in the living room has more to do with your decision than your headstrong grandmother."

Marilyn ground her teeth together. Was she that apparent? "Casey, don't read anything into Dusty and me spending time together. True, he's made life more interesting since he arrived, but I promised Gran I wouldn't leave until I got to know him better, that's all. You know, so I'd feel better about him being here. I mean, I can't leave Gran living with a total stranger."

"So stay and find out what he's all about."

"The thing is, I can't see us together. He's searching for . . . something he lost and I'm off to a bright new future." Marilyn shook her head again, this time with purpose. "No, I just can't see anything more than friendship between us."

"So he's less a stranger, more a handsome friend?"

Marilyn forced a convincing tone. "Exactly. A friend."

Casey burst out laughing.

"What?"

"Honey, you should see yourself. You're face gets all soft when you talk about him, yet you're determined to ignore the fact that you're interested."

"Well, you did say he's handsome."

"And as soon as that fact gets out, all the single women in Paineville will find one excuse after another to visit Ruby Sue. Then where will you be?"

Marilyn frowned. Where would she be? In Charlotte working on building a name in real estate? Or right here, standing in line with Kitty and the rest of the single woman population vying for Dusty's affection? A twinge of jealousy twisted in her.

Ruby Sue hung up the phone and brushed past Marilyn to push the swinging kitchen door open. "Ty, get in here." Her lined face glowed and her smile stretched from ear to ear.

Ty barreled into the kitchen seconds later, followed by Dusty. "What's wrong?"

"Nothin's wrong, everything's right. Gabe's comin'

home for good and bringin' my great-granddaughter with him."

She grabbed Marilyn close, then tugged Ty and Casey into a tight group hug. "My entire brood will be home."

Marilyn gently pulled back and cast a glance at her brother, who smiled at his wife, eyes shining with love. Another stab of envy pierced Marilyn. Along with the never ending guilt. She didn't want Gran hurt again.

Marilyn stepped away from the group and glanced at Dusty. He propped his shoulder against the door jam, arms crossed over his broad chest, observing the familial bliss before him. His smile dimmed a fraction when he looked at her. He must have noticed the tension on her face. With a slight shift of his head, he beckoned her into the other room. She willingly followed. Too willingly.

He leveled her with his too-astute gaze. "I thought you'd be happy about your brother coming home."

She placed a reassuring hand on his arm, the unmistakable charge of excitement skittering through her. Then she yanked her hand back at the feel of the hard corded muscle beneath his shirt sleeve, annoyed at her immediate response to him. She had to resolutely ignore Dusty's rugged strength. A strength she sensed she could rely on. It was way too soon to be thinking in that direction.

"Oh, I am happy. It's . . . I don't want to hurt Gran when I leave."

Dusty considered her for a moment, but his poker face didn't reveal if he felt the same attraction that she did. "We're going for a walk, you and me. The fresh air should help you sort things out."

Marilyn headed to the foyer to get her jacket while Dusty poked his head into the kitchen to tell her family they'd be outside.

She stepped onto the porch as she shrugged on her jacket, the gusty wind whipping stands of hair around her face.

"Kinda brisk out here," Dusty said as he joined her.

"It feels wonderful." They walked down the steps together. "I love this time of year. The leaves changing color. The chill in the mornings and evenings. Especially all the different scents in the air."

"Not to mention your grandmother's cooking."

"That too."

Marilyn led them down the driveway to a path that ran along the property line. Dry leaves crunched under their boots and an occasional bird scattered from the trees.

"How long have you lived here with your grandmother?"

"Just a few months now. Gran's lived here about six years. Ty built the house, but she lived alone until her health started giving her trouble. That's when I moved back."

"So where does this other brother of yours live?"

"Florida. He married his college sweetheart and they moved to Tampa after the wedding. He's in a law firm there."

"So why is he coming back?"

"Cindy, his wife, died five years ago. I think he wanted to stay there so Emily would feel a connection to her mom. I'm betting that it isn't working. It seems they've been coming home more frequently lately."

"That's great, the way your family rallies around each other."

"We've always been tight."

They turned a bend in the path and came upon a broken-down mobile home nestled under a crowding of trees. Lopsided steps sagged under the front door. Rust spots marred the chipped paint. Marilyn stopped walking and wrapped her arms over her chest. Despite her intention not to, she blurted out, "This is why I want to leave."

Dusty stared at the run-down trailer. "Wouldn't it just be easier to have it hauled off?"

She held his eyes with her gaze.

"Okay, want to explain?"

"We grew up in that trailer. My parents split when we were little. Gran raised us the best she could, but to most people we were the poor kids living in the trailer. And that's putting it nicely.

"When Ty bought this property, he moved our home to this spot. In fact, he lived in the trailer until he married Casey. Guess he meant it to be a reminder to us all that we'd moved up in the world. We may not be poor, but we're still Banners."

"I see. You have something to prove."

"Don't we all?"

"Yeah. I think we do." Marilyn shrugged, not ready to get into this conversation. Not when it meant tapping into the deep underlying hurt she shared with no one.

Banners never amounted to much and never will.

The words still haunted her. She turned from the

dilapidated scene before her. "C'mon. Dinner should be ready."

Minutes later they entered the house through the kitchen door.

"Here you are," Ruby Sue scolded. "I was thinkin' we might have to start without you two."

Dusty winked at her. "You don't think we'd miss one of your meals, do you?"

Marilyn gaped as her normally unflappable grandmother blushed. She actually got all flustered at Dusty's compliment?

"You're good," she muttered under her breath as she passed him to join the others in the dining room.

"Don't you forget it."

Pleasant chills tingled over Marilyn at his confident tone. She'd never seen anyone handle Gran as easily as he did.

After the prayer, Marilyn watched her family chatter about Gabe's homecoming. Ruby Sue's eyes shined, and years seemed to fall away from her face.

"So, have you set a date yet?" Ruby Sue asked Marilyn.

"Date?" What was her grandmother talking about?

Ty chuckled. "Ruby, you really need to use some subtlety here. Poor Dusty doesn't know what he's getting into."

"Dusty? Oh, you thought I was . . . Tyrone Banner, watch your tongue, presuming you know what you're talkin' about."

"You are the matchmaker." Ty nodded at Dusty. "Sorry, man. Hey, at least she didn't have the minister waiting in the living room."

"No problem," Dusty answered as he raised a questioning brow at Marilyn.

"Running family joke," she reminded him.

"Well, you're wrong on this one, Ty," Ruby Sue continued. "I'm talkin' about your sister. Marilyn's plannin' on moving away."

Ty laid his fork on the table. "What? Since when?"

Marilyn heaved a heavy sigh, knowing her brother was about to let her have it with both barrels. "Since recently. I've been offered a job in Charlotte and I'm going to take it."

"Why? You've got something good going on right here."

"I could have a better thing going up there."

"Marilyn, we talked about this. You know you won't be happy somewhere else." Ty resorted to his big brother, disciplinarian tone like he always did when he didn't like what he heard.

Her anger was piqued. "How do you know? I've never been anywhere else." She sighed at her brother's perplexed expression. "I just want to give it a try. You went out on your own for a while. Gabe has. Now I want my turn."

"But now? With Gabe coming home?"

"What better time? Gran will be busy fussing over Emily. And I know you and Casey want kids. Now is the time."

"But—"

"Ty," Casey cut in, gently placing her hand over his. "Let it go. She's made her decision."

Ty looked at his wife and the tension faded from his face. He turned to Marilyn. "You're serious?"

"Yes."

"See, the girl's got her mind set," Ruby Sue muttered. "Only one thing will change that stubborn will of hers."

"Oh yeah?" Marilyn laughed at her grandmother's totally convinced posture. "And what would that be?"

Ruby Sue smiled. She glanced pointedly at Dusty, then back to Marilyn. "Love."

Chapter Six

"Paineville Realty. Marilyn Banner speaking."

"Marilyn. Max Gleason here. Checking in to confirm the date when you'll be joining us."

Marilyn's grip on the receiver tightened. This was the call she was waiting for. "Mr. Gleason. You've definitely been on my mind. I've had some family—issues come up so I haven't been able to get back to you."

"Nothing critical I hope."

"No. Thanks for your concern."

"We're like a big family here, so I understand. But I have to ask, have you chosen a date?"

She made quick mental calculations. The festival started this weekend. Then there was the holiday. She'd be free after that. "How about the weekend after Thanksgiving?"

"I was hoping to move the date up in order for you to meet some prospective clients I have lined up. We really don't want to hesitate on the deal."

Marilyn held her breath, wondering if the unspoken implication would ruin her chances of making a good start. She understood how important timing was with buying clients. Especially this time of year, with the holidays close by.

Before she had a chance to question him, Mr. Gleason spoke again. "Why don't you drive up the day after Thanksgiving? I have a client that will be here for the long weekend. We can work with him, then you can settle in over the remainder of the weekend and start the following Monday."

She sucked in a breath. If she really wanted to impress the client she'd have to get there early, which meant leaving Thanksgiving Day. Gran's favorite holiday. She'd be so disappointed over not having her entire family together.

Even though Marilyn made it no secret that she planned on leaving, that particular day could cause problems at home. Still . . .

"That's fine, Mr. Gleason," she answered, ignoring the guilty hitch in her chest at letting Gran down.

"Good. I'll be in touch with the details of your move."

Marilyn replaced the phone. Two weeks. Just like that, she'd made her decision. After weighing the pros and cons. After considering her future. She sighed. Ruby Sue didn't want her to go, and Marilyn knew that would be the case when she made her decision, but imagining the letdown on her grandmother's face wrenched her heartstrings.

Now Gabe and Emily would be coming home to stay. And as much as Marilyn wanted to spend time with her niece, she really needed to strike out on her own.

And then there was Dusty. Her mixed up emotions didn't really know how to handle the man. She was attracted—oh yeah, she was attracted. Granted, they hadn't known each other long, but she knew that the attraction simmering between them went deeper than just the surface. At least for her.

But long-term? Did Dusty even think about the future while he dealt with his own problems? Besides which, he hadn't expressed a committed interest in her. What was she thinking?

Now, after years of waiting for 'her time,' she shuddered. Go for her dreams? Hang around and see what happened with her family? Wait to see if Dusty made his move? The answer hovered closely, right within her grasp. *Try, or you'll always regret it if you don't.*

Dropping her chin into cupped hands, she muttered, "Be careful what you wish for."

By noon, Marilyn had completely lost her concentration. She packed up and headed home for lunch, deciding that one of Ruby Sue's roast beef sandwiches would put her in a better frame of mind.

She let herself in the front door, just as Dusty walked by the foyer, headed to the living room. He carried a large tray loaded with teacups, saucers, a large teapot, and a plate of some sort of finger sandwiches.

She stared at him, wide eyed.

"Don't ask," he warned with a grimace before stepping into the living room.

Marilyn closed in behind him, watching as he lowered the tray onto the coffee table in front of the couch. Six women including her grandmother sat around the room, crochet hooks and yarn in hand. She watched, astounded at how he worked the room. These ladies didn't have a chance of leaving today with their hearts intact.

A warm fuzzy feeling enveloped her and she grinned. Each month the Silver Butterflies, as the ladies called themselves, got together to create different crafts. Today, they were crocheting butterflies that would be sold as Christmas ornaments. Marilyn knew that each year the ornaments sold out the first day of the festival. The money went to various charitable organizations. In return, people had their very own piece of Paineville tradition to hang on the Christmas tree.

"Marilyn, join us. I'm sure Dusty wouldn't mind fetching another cup of tea."

"No, that's okay, Gran. I'm going into the kitchen for a bite to eat. Dusty, care to join me?"

He flashed her a lopsided grin and her heart melted. "I aim to please."

Marilyn entered the kitchen, her eyebrows raised at her grandmother's normally tidy kitchen. If she didn't know better, Marilyn would have thought a hurricane had whipped through the room. Hurricane Dusty, to be exact.

"Any smart remarks?" Dusty asked without preamble as he strode into the room.

"No. Not me. I know better than to come between a man and his . . . er . . . teatime."

"Smart woman."

"At least you aren't wearing an apron."

"Ruby Sue didn't have one in my size."

She laughed, picturing her grandmother trying to tie a frilly apron around Dusty. "So what are you doing?"

"Your grandmother had this tea party thing lined up and she sent me out to pick up the ladies that couldn't drive. By the time we returned, she had the living room all fixed up, had most of the food ready, and she looked so tired I thought she'd drop on the spot."

Marilyn's frowned in concern. "She didn't mention anything to me. I hope she's not feeling sick again."

"Don't think so. But with the festival and this monthly group meeting, she's doing too much."

Guilt engulfed her again. Shouldn't she be the one here helping her grandmother? Instead of obsessing over her move to another city?

"Anyway, I sent her into the other room with her friends and took over the kitchen duties. A chef, even just for sandwiches, I am not."

Marilyn picked up a delicate cucumber triangle and examined it. "You made this?"

"Not entirely. Ruby Sue had all the crusts off the bread before I arrived on the scene." He held up a tea bag by the string and smiled broadly. "I can boil water."

She laughed. "You know, for a man who claims to have been such a hard nose in the business world, this is actually sweet."

Dusty turned away, but Marilyn had already seen the grin he tried to hide at her compliment.

"Besides," he continued, "since I left home, I miss being spoiled by my grandmother. Yours will have to do."

"If she's anything like Gran, we're in deep trouble."

"She hides her meddling behind this really sweet

façade. But I'm on to her." Dusty chuckled. "She and Ruby Sue would make quite a team."

"Speaking of sweet, don't you need to serve dessert?"

"Oh, man. I almost forgot." He swung around to the counter in search of another serving dish.

Marilyn walked to the cabinet and removed a tray large enough for the cheese and fruit Danishes and set it on the counter. "Let me arrange the dessert, okay?"

"Thanks." He handed her a box from the Pastry Palace.

"Did Gran order these? She usually makes desert herself."

"I stopped in town and picked this up."

"This harvest festival has really got her going. She thinks she has the energy of a twenty-year-old."

"That's why I bought pastries, to give her a break."

Once again he'd managed to capture her heart. "Thanks, Dusty. I really mean it."

He waved off her compliment. "Let me take this to the ladies."

Marilyn followed him from the room, grinning at such a rugged man serving a bunch of petite older ladies and not worrying about being teased. Her appreciation of the man was growing in leaps and bounds.

"So I'm thinkin' that a holiday wedding would be nice. Keep everyone in a festive mood."

Marilyn froze when she heard her grandmother's voice, stopping short of bumping into Dusty, who had also halted just before the archway into the living room.

"When do you think the wedding will take place?"

"Soon, I hope. I'm not gettin' any younger. These younguns today need a little nudge in the right direction."

"I suppose Marilyn is leery, what with her mother's example and all."

The room went deathly silent. When Ruby Sue spoke again, her tone was quiet, but firm. "Marilyn is nothin' like her mama in that respect. And anyone with half a brain could see that."

"And we're all proud of Marilyn," came Molly's dear voice. "She's done real well for herself."

The chatter picked up in volume. To her surprise, Marilyn found her fists filled with the fabric of Dusty's chambray shirt.

"You can let go now," he instructed in a calm tone.

She released her tight grip, smoothing out the fabric with jerky strokes.

"I'm going in," he said in a stage whisper before entering the room. Marilyn high-tailed it back to the kitchen.

She strode to the sink, to stare out the window. She would *not* let careless words hurt her. She would *not* cry. She had grown up to be successful, which was so much more than her mother had ever accomplished. She would *not* let the past and the expectations of others crush her resolve.

With a trembling sigh, she reached up to brush a lone tear from her cheek.

By the time Dusty returned minutes later, Marilyn had regained control over her emotions and started to tidy up.

"Hey, you okay?" Dusty asked. "I mean, about their topic of conversation back there?"

"Sure. Happens all the time. I'm used to it."

"Used to what? Your grandmother's blatant match-making or people talking about your mother?"

"Both, I guess. Look, Dusty, I appreciate your concern, but I just can't talk about Mom."

He silently watched her for a heartbeat, then nodded. "Fair enough. And if you don't mind, I'd like to skip the wedding talk."

She released a breath, followed by a laugh, grateful for his levity. "Deal."

Dusty laid the tray on the counter and turned to face her. Marilyn stood on the opposite side of the room, aware that if she didn't keep her distance, she might want the comfort of his arms around her. Instead, she changed the subject.

"You've mentioned your grandmother, but not the rest of your family. Where do they live?"

Dusty pointed to some leftover sandwiches. "You said you were hungry. Eat up."

"I'll eat, you talk."

She cleared a place at the table and fixed herself a cup of Earl Grey tea before sitting down. "Go ahead. I'm waiting."

"Don't you have a house to sell or something?"

"Nope. I'm free this afternoon."

"Don't you want to join the ladies?"

"I'd rather sit here and talk about you. And why you're trying so hard to avoid the subject."

He sighed and joined her at the table. "I don't want to push you away. I just don't know what you want to hear."

"Start with folks, siblings, whatever you feel is pertinent."

"Okay. My folks and grandparents live in Tennessee. My grandmother is from around here, but she moved away when she married my grandfather."

"Your grandmother, the meddler?"

He grinned. "That's the one. Anyway, I grew up in a very happy, very busy family. One older brother, one younger sister. They're both married and I have nieces and nephews."

"How come you never married?"

"I could ask you the same thing."

"You could, but we're talking about you."

He paused, his eyes never meeting hers. "I never found the right woman."

"Do you want kids?"

"Someday."

"When you figure out what you want out of life?"

He grinned and looked directly at her. "Oh, darlin', I know what I want."

Her eyes widened at his teasing tone.

"But there's nothing wrong with stepping back and re-evaluating," he continued. "We can't all be single-minded."

"True."

"I hear a 'but' . . ."

"But you really do know what you want," she told him. "The question is, have you pursued it?"

"Okay, Professor Banner. If you're so smart, tell me what I want."

"You want to write music."

He stared at the table, fingering the napkin within his reach.

"So I hit home?"

"Yeah. There's just one problem."

"Which is."

"I can't make myself settle down long enough to see if I still have the gift."

"So that's why you've been keeping busy with my grandmother? As an excuse not to face what's really going on?"

"Realtor and shrink. Must come in handy."

"At times." On everyone but herself. "What's your worst fear?" she pestered.

He sat back in his chair and frowned. "That the words won't ever come. That I won't ever again hear a new melody I created.

"It's weird, I hear my songs on the radio, knowing that at one point I had more words in me than I could get down on paper. Now? I have nothing."

"Have you sat down and tried?" She knew the answer, but wanted to hear it from him. In her mind, the vivid picture of Dusty, alone at the piano with such a look of despair on his face, tugged at her heartstrings.

"I—tried." His expression clouded. "It goes deeper, Marilyn, beyond just getting the words down. I need time to figure it out, so I'm running all over town, keeping busy, till I hear the music in my mind."

"Maybe you need to slow down and listen."

When he didn't reply, Marilyn realized her good intentions hadn't lifted the dejected expression from Dusty's face. She could relate. She'd been disappointed in her life, only in her case she kept waiting for her mother to come home. And the woman never did. How devastated would Dusty be if he never used his gift again?

"Tell you what. I won't badger you with any more

personal questions today. Let's finish cleaning up this mess."

He narrowed his eyes. "Why?"

"I might need a song written especially for me someday. So you'll owe me."

Dusty stared at her for long moments, but didn't move.

Marilyn swallowed, hoping she hadn't just made things worse for him.

Two days later, Marilyn greeted Gabe and Emily as they returned home to much fanfare, hugs, and kisses. She left work early and picked up Casey at her store, Crafty Creations, so they could ride to Ruby Sue's house together. Ty headed home from the construction site to enter the thrall of hugs and kisses. Ruby Sue flitted around the room, always returning to Emily to touch her face or stroke her hair, before gravitating to Gabe, smiling her biggest grin.

After the initial hugs, Marilyn was caught off guard by Gabe's appearance. Since his last visit he'd lost some weight and worry lines creased his forehead. Even Emily acted a bit subdued. Later, when they were alone, Marilyn planned on finding out what, exactly, was bothering them.

For now, the family gathered in the kitchen while Ruby Sue laid out a small spread and everyone got reacquainted. Marilyn joined in the revelry, even as her stomach knotted with uncertainty. After she moved, how long would it be until she sat with the entire family assembled under one roof? And how would she break the news that she had a definite date of departure? She mentally shook her head to clear the plaguing thoughts so she could enjoy this time with her loved ones.

Gabe tousled Emily's toffee-brown hair. "I've already registered Emily for school here. She starts tomorrow."

"Oh, Dad, can't I have a few days off? I want to spend time with Gran."

His somber eyes narrowed. "After your antics at the old school, you need to get back into class right away." When Emily opened her mouth to argue, Gabe cut her off. "No changing my mind."

Emily stared at the floor, silent.

"So Gabe, what are your plans?" Ty asked, watching both his niece and brother with an uneasy gaze.

"I'm not sure. I need some time to think about that. Maybe I can bum a job from you."

"What about your law practice?" Casey asked.

"I left the firm. Permanently."

All eyes went to Gabe, but he keep staring into his coffee cup.

"There's always plenty to do around here," Ruby Sue informed him, not one to let a life crisis keep her from recruiting new help. "And the Harvest Festival starts this weekend. I can use an extra pair of hands."

"I thought Dusty took care of all your errands," Marilyn teased.

"He can't do everything."

"Dusty?" Gabe asked.

Ty rolled his eyes. "Gran's boarder."

"Oh, right. Marilyn mentioned him when I called. Do you need him to stay now that we're home?"

" 'Course he can stay. There's room for everyone in this big house."

"Well, actually, Gran, there's not," Marilyn reminded her. "But Emily can room with me until I leave."

Silence filtered through the room.

"When do you leave?" Ruby Sue asked.

Marilyn swallowed against the knot that had suddenly formed in her throat. "Two weeks. I'll probably head out Thanksgiving Day."

"Well, I'm having dinner," came her grandmother's stubborn response. "You're welcome to join us if you can fit us into your schedule."

Marilyn cringed at Gran's blunt tone, then glanced around the room. She knew her grandmother hid her hurt behind her curt words, but she wasn't so sure about the rest of the clan. Ty glared at her, Casey smiled in commiseration, Gabe frowned, and Emily came over to hug her. Suddenly, she felt like an outsider in the one place she'd always found love and acceptance.

"I'll bunk with you till then, Aunt Marilyn."

Ruby Sue moved to the stove to pour warm water from the kettle into her teacup. "When Dusty decides to move on, we'll have more room."

Ty, standing by the counter, glanced out the window. "That might happen sooner than you think."

"What?" Marilyn sprinted around the table to look out the window. Dusty strode across the yard, his duffel in hand, headed in the direction the trailer.

"Oh, no," she whispered.

"What's that boy up to?" Ruby Sue demanded.

"I don't know, but I plan on finding out." Marilyn grabbed a jacket from the hook by the back door and headed out after Dusty. She'd broken into a jog before she caught up to him, a few hundred feet from the mobile trailer.

"Just what are you doing?"

Dusty dropped his bag and swung around to face her. A smile lit his lips. "Checking out my new digs."

"Here?" She gestured helplessly toward the rusted-out structure.

"Sure, why not? Your brother said it was livable."

"Why?"

"Look, your brother and his daughter need rooms. I don't mind moving out. As long as I'm close to Ruby Sue's cooking."

"Dusty, you're a paying boarder. You can't live here."

"Why not? You all did. Ty did. What difference does it make?"

What difference did it make? None to him. Everything to her.

Again, an unbidden memory assailed Marilyn. She remembered the night of her senior prom. She stood outside the trailer, anxiously waiting for her date. He'd been a quiet boy, the first to really seem genuinely interested in her.

He never showed up that night, a night so filled with promise, so filled with expectation.

Ty had come home about an hour after the dance officially started, finding her sitting on the steps, brushing tears from her cheeks.

She found out later that Ty had had a 'conversation' with the boy. Turns out that when the boy's father realized who her family was, he'd forbade the boy from picking Marilyn up that night. Seems he'd spent some time chasing Marilyn's mother, who had refused the man's advances, and he didn't want his son around that same type of woman.

Marilyn groaned inwardly at the memory. Same type of woman? She'd only been sixteen years old at the time. Still, the rejection hurt.

Her thoughts spiraled back to the here and now. She covered her old pain by trying logic on Dusty. "The trailer isn't that well insulated—you'll freeze now that the temperatures are dropping. I know that from experience." How many times had she curled into a tight ball under thin blankets trying to keep warm?

"Ty said he put in a space heater. I'll be fine."

"The place needs a good cleaning."

"I can clean."

Why was he being so difficult? "There's no piano."

He ignored her jibe. "I have a keyboard. It'll do."

She stared at him, then at the aging trailer. Rust patches ate holes through the paint. The shaky steps listed to one side. The whole pathetic structure seemed to sag under the elements of nature and age. Yet Dusty's staying here was a lot closer than his moving to town.

She glanced back at him, seeing steely determination burning in his eyes. "Are you sure?" she whispered.

Dusty moved beside her. "Marilyn, this is just a place to rest my head, to hang my hat between errands. I don't have any memories of this place. It can't hurt me. And it can only hurt you if you let it."

Tears stung the insides of her lids. Why did she let this place have such a hold over her? It was just that, a place. She didn't have to live here.

Yet her mother's voice continued to haunt her. She

recalled overhearing the final conversation between her mother and Gran. *"I'm leaving, Mama. This place ain't good enough for me. I've got to go out and—"*

"Chase after some no-account dream?"

"I can't stay."

"You have younguns."

"They're better off without me."

Yes, they were better off, she thought with anger. Ruby Sue had been the better mother. She held the family together through all kinds of odds.

"You don't have to come inside," Dusty said quietly.

"And you can't clean this place alone."

He regarded her for a long time, then offered his hand. "Okay. Help me."

She stared at the trailer again. Maybe, here with Dusty, she could permanently clean away that past.

When she nodded, he grasped her hand and led her up the rickety steps to the wooden deck. He pulled the keys from his jacket pocket to unlock the door. He turned the knob, but nothing happened. With a heave, he shouldered the door. A brief hesitation followed before the structure gave way, propelling him into the room. He stumbled inside. "Need that fixed," he muttered.

Marilyn stepped over the threshold, waiting for something to physically knock the memories from her. Instead, cold air greeted her. Nothing else.

A thin film of dust blanketed the furnishings. A slightly musty, closed-up odor permeated the room— nothing that opening the windows wouldn't cure.

"This isn't half bad," Dusty commented as he surveyed the small living area before heading to the back to check out the bedrooms.

Marilyn wandered into the kitchen and turned on the tap. Memories of Ruby Sue busy at work in here eased her mind as clean water ran into the sink. Next she checked the refrigerator. The electricity worked.

Dusty ambled into the tiny kitchen. She turned to face him and her grin froze in place. His broad shoulders filled the doorway. The tight quarters forced him into her personal space as he stepped near her. Butterflies tangled in her stomach, warning her that he captivated her like no other man had ever done. His wolfish smile chilled her skin, but the banked heat in his eyes set her blood boiling.

"Things working in here?" he asked with a lazy drawl.

She swallowed. "Looks good."

He rolled up his sleeves and peered at her with intense emotion. "I'm going outside to get my bag, then I'm starting the clean-up campaign. Care to join me?"

"Sure. The family won't mind if I'm gone for a while. This way they can crab some more about me."

"What happened?"

"I told them I'm leaving Thanksgiving Day."

Dusty stared at her for long moments. "Bet that didn't go over well."

"Actually, Gran took it in stride. She's not happy, but she won't try to stop me."

"Did you expect anything less?"

"Truthfully, I expected more resistance."

"Look, you've made it clear you want to leave. Guess Ruby Sue's accepted it." He left the trailer to grab his bag, not expanding on his thoughts.

Marilyn tried to ignore her disappointment at his words. Gran hadn't argued. So she should be happy, right? It was like getting the older woman's blessing. So why wasn't she elated?

Shaking off her thoughts, Marilyn pulled her hair into a ponytail and busied herself at the sink, adding soap she found under the counter to the hot water. Dusty turned on the radio in the living area. A popular country song set the cleaning tempo. Marilyn scrubbed and scrubbed, determined not to allow one speck of dirt to linger.

As she wiped the cloth over an aluminum window frame, her fingernail snagged the hook, taking the acrylic with it. "Ow," she cried, jumping back to cradle her hand in the other.

Dusty ran in. "What's wrong?"

"I broke my nail."

"The way you screamed, I thought you cut yourself."

"This isn't good. I'll have to call Arlette to fix it and there's no telling when she can fit me in." It had taken almost three days to reschedule her canceled hair appointment.

"It's not the end of the world."

She frowned at him. "Had any nails ripped from your fingers lately?"

Dusty wisely backed off. "I'm gonna finish the other room."

"Good idea."

Marilyn hurried to the bathroom but couldn't find a Band-Aid. She searched the room for anything resembling a bandage, but there were no first aid supplies. She headed back to the kitchen. Dusty leaned against the door jamb, a roll of black duct tape dangling from his fingers. "Will this help?"

She gaped at the tape, then at him. "You're kidding, right?"

"Hey, if it covers your finger, it works."

"Guys really do use duct tape for everything."

He took her fingers gently in his. Jolts of liquid heat skittered up her arm. She stood completely still, trying not to show how much his touch affected her. Trying to keep her chest from noticeably rising with each labored breath.

"It doesn't look that bad," he said, his focus totally on her finger and not her heated reaction to him. "You still have part of the nail on there."

"That's my real nail."

He looked at her, apparently perplexed at the concept of acrylic nails. "Okay. So we cover it up until you can get it fixed." He wrapped a small bit of tape over her finger, then held up his handiwork for her inspection.

"A real fashion statement," she grumbled.

"I don't know how you work with those fake nails anyway. Don't they get in the way?"

"Of what?"

"Everything."

"But it's the style."

"Who cares about the style. Just be yourself."

Marilyn started laughing, and to her horror, couldn't stop. Here she tried so hard to look uptown and Dusty thought it got in the way. Lately, the way she looked at her life was at odds with what others saw.

"What's so funny?"

"My image. Ripped off by a nail."

He frowned.

"Never mind." She'd worked so hard to look a certain way, to exude a business persona. She'd taken great pains to learn which were the right cosmetics for her skin tone. Which hair style was trendy. For what? She'd ended up back here in the trailer with a man who saw no difference. He only saw the real her.

"Am I missing something?"

"Dusty, I'm a professional. I need to look a certain way."

"Marilyn, you're beautiful. No matter what you choose to be, you'll always look good."

She purposely looked around the room, hoping the heat she felt warming her face didn't tip Dusty off to how much his compliment meant to her. "I suppose you're going to say it's what's inside that counts."

"It's the past, Marilyn. Don't go stirring up trouble that isn't there."

"This coming from a man who doesn't know what to do with his own life?"

That quieted him momentarily. "You're right. Who am I to give you advice?"

Marilyn bit her tongue, wishing she could take back her waspish words. She hadn't meant to be hurtful, but she'd been bombarded by so many new and confusing emotions today that she hadn't watched her tongue. Before she could say anything to soften the blow, Dusty walked into the other room.

They finished cleaning in silence, right until dinnertime.

Marilyn broke the wall of silence that had risen between them. "Are you coming up to the house? I'm sure Gran has dinner ready."

"Give me a few minutes to shower."

She grabbed her jacket from the couch. She couldn't stand the silent treatment any longer. Not that she didn't deserve it. "Um, Dusty, I'm sorry I snapped at you. I guess making my decision and springing it on everyone today has made me a little stressed."

He approached her, closing in the gap that seemed to have spread between them like a valley. She searched his gaze, trying to read his expression. His blue eyes revealed understanding, and to her surprise and pleasure, the heat from earlier still lingered. Her heart pounded as she waited to see what he would do next. Would he kiss her and end the rift between them?

Instead, he said, "Hey, you were right. I need to settle my own life before I start handing out advice. Don't worry about it."

But she did. All the way back to the house and all through the dinner that Dusty didn't show up for.

Chapter Seven

The next two days passed in a blur of activity. During that time, Dusty had been forefront in Marilyn's mind. The smallest little thing, like hearing a love song on the radio or glancing out the window to watch dusk settle over the mountains, made her feel warm and unsettled, much the way she felt whenever she was with him.

Marilyn had taken a few hours off from work to pack some belongings, as well as help Ruby Sue with pressing issues involving the festival, and somehow managed to end up in Dusty's truck, traveling around town as he ran errands. He didn't mention the day at the trailer, so Marilyn avoided bringing it up. Instead, they politely avoided stepping on each other's toes.

Late Friday afternoon, they arrived at their last errand, picking up a delivery of hay from Densler's Farm. Dusty used the forklift to place the bales beside the truck. He returned, donning heavy work gloves to finish the job.

Being outdoors agreed with the man. She couldn't help but admire his rugged good looks, from his dark tousled hair to the sharp, masculine angles of his face. His muscular build superbly filled out his faded flannel shirt, worn jeans, and work boots. He rolled the shirt sleeves to just below his elbows. Just staring at him made her mouth dry.

"Didn't you bring any gloves?" He gazed pointedly at her hands.

"No. I didn't think of it. It's been a while since I did manual labor."

"Then watch your fancy fingernails."

She held up her hands and wiggled her fingers for inspection. "I had the acrylic nails removed. I decided to go all natural for the festival."

He grinned. "Next you'll be telling me you've thrown all your business suits away and replaced them with jeans and sweatshirts."

She looked down at that exact attire. "Don't get carried away," she warned. "A girl can only give up one fashion statement at a time."

"Well, the nails are a good start."

"Thanks for the critique, but we need to get this delivery back to the park."

Dusty shook his head. "I still can't believe how much work your grandmother gets out of everyone. Today she had your brother building some kind of a big platform and he went right along with it."

"He falls into line, just like the rest of us."

"Yeah, well he was laughing the entire time he hammered nails. I got the distinct impression something was up."

She shrugged. "It couldn't be anything more than a

place to showcase all the jams and preserves the ladies have made. Or maybe the base for a dunk tank. That would tickle Ty's sense of humor."

"Isn't it too cold for a dunk tank?"

"Hey, you've got to go with the flow."

"As long as you think so. Seemed more . . . outlandish to me."

"You worry too much."

He chuckled. "Now you have me mixed up with you. You're the worrier, unless you've turned over a new leaf."

"No. I try to stop worrying when it comes to my family. I can't control them, so there's no point getting stressed over their actions."

"Really? Letting go of the past?"

Surprised by his observation, she glanced over at him. Had she decided to put the past behind her? Or, more correctly, the past her mother had predestined by leaving them behind? For once, thinking about her mother didn't hurt so badly. Maybe Dusty was right. Maybe she was letting go.

"So, how about you? Any progress in writing music?"

"I haven't had a spare minute to sit down and write, even if I wanted to. Ruby Sue has me driving all over town."

"Once the festival is over, you won't have an excuse."

"I know," he answered, his voice low and discouraged. "So give me a few more days' reprieve."

Marilyn bent over to slide her fingers under the end of a bale. The hay prickled against her soft skin. "Okay. For now. Let's get the hay loaded."

Dusty lowered the trunk gate. "Slave driver," he dead-panned.

Marilyn grasped the wire wrapped around the hay and helped him heave the ball into the truck bed. With Dusty taking the brunt of the weight, they loaded the inventory quickly. Working in unison, they didn't take long to load most of the truck.

She watched Dusty climb onto the tailgate to arrange the bales, allowing room for the last few. His muscles flexed beneath his shirt as he worked effortlessly with the bundles. She, on the other hand, couldn't help staring and wondering just how firm those muscles really were.

"Who's going to use all this hay?" he asked.

"Huh, what?" She shifted her glance from his chest to his questioning gaze. "Oh, um, if I remember correctly, they'll use some to spread around the booths, you know, for ambiance. And for the ponies."

"Sounds messy."

"Yeah, but if you're not on the clean-up committee, don't worry about it."

"I just might be on the list if your grandmother has her way."

"I have connections, I'll make sure you get out of that detail."

"Okay. What else is going on with the hay?"

"They'll make rows of seating in front of the stage so people can relax during the entertainment. By the way, did you recommend Dixie Highway for the lead act?"

"Yes. I told you, they were very good."

"Really? That good?"

"Good enough for a record deal, if an exec hears them and wants to sign them on."

"Which you aren't doing anymore."

"Right. I'm not doing it anymore."

Marilyn watched his face, searching for any telltale signs that he might change his mind and go back to his former life. She saw nothing to give any indication that he might be tempted to return to the business aspect of music. After all, he made no bones about the fact that he'd been burned. And after spending time with him, she really believed that he didn't want to go back to that life. He only wanted to write music.

And once he found his way back to his true calling, which she had no doubt he'd accomplish, he'd probably move on. Either way, they'd go in separate directions.

"Last one, let's go," Dusty called to her.

Marilyn shook off her thoughts and helped Dusty heave the last bale onto the tailgate. As they tossed it up, the bale toppled off the pile and rolled toward her.

"Watch out!" Dusty propelled Marilyn out of harm's way.

She tumbled into the dirt and landed hard, stray bits of hay clinging to her clothes and hair. She flailed, sputtering as Dusty landed on her. "I can't believe you pushed me down."

He leveled himself on his elbows and gazed down at her, his eyes fiery. "For the record, I didn't push you down. I was trying to keep you from getting hurt just now."

She wiggled, pushing against his solid shoulders. At least she got her wish. She knew that his muscles were gloriously firm. Artistically sculpted, to be exact. And all within her reach as his weight rested atop her.

She moved her gaze to meet his, caught up in the heat of his body and the fire in his gaze. She didn't want to move, didn't want this moment to end. She'd hate herself later for melting under his touch, but right now, all her fantasies about Dusty dimmed in the hard reality of his body pressed against hers.

"Are you sure you're okay?"

His husky words, spoken so gently, dragged her back to her senses. Apparently he was affected as much as she. And she was afraid of where this might lead.

So she pushed again, adding a caustic tone to her voice. "I won't know until you get off of me. Would you move already?"

He grinned that self-satisfied grin of his. Didn't he realize she was intentionally dismissing him? "I kinda like it here."

"Move."

"Okay, okay, don't get all huffy."

When he reluctantly moved away, a chill swept over her traitorous body. She missed the dangerous warmth of his lean body, the feminine thrill that shimmied over her at his touch.

He offered her a hand up.

She took it.

Once standing, she dusted off her jeans, wincing when she bent her wrist.

"You see, you *are* hurt."

"I just twisted my wrist. It's no big deal."

"I'll decide that." Dusty gently took her hand and placed it over his open palm. He squeezed around the bone. His probing fingers found tender areas, but no pain. But his touch definitely brought a now familiar tingling in her stomach. "You might get a little bruising."

"I can handle it." But Dusty's concern and intimate touch had her wondering if she could handle him. She let out a breath and looked up to find him blatantly staring back at her.

The world stopped around her. All her focus centered on Dusty. His eyes, filled with fire and promise, probed hers. His scent, tangy and definitely male, teased her. And his possessive touch stole her breath away.

His gaze moved to her lips, signaling his desire to kiss her. And she wanted him to. Wanted to feel his lips against hers, to feel that topsy-turvy, world-careening-out-of-control sensation she felt only when Dusty kissed her. If only he'd make his move . . .

When he hesitated too long, she stood on tiptoe as he lowered his head, grabbing his shoulders to yank him to her. This time she met him full on, not letting him take the lead. She wanted to taste him, hungering to be swept away in the passion of this man. Only this man. A man whose touch left her quaking and wishing for dreams she'd never allowed herself to imagine before. His touch left her dizzy with anticipation. And she found herself wanting one man only, as never before in her life.

Why did she react this way to him? Longing and breathless sensations were not part of her life. She'd never met a man who made her heart dance, her pulse skitter, or her senses spin out of control.

Surprised by her actions, Marilyn slowly returned

to her senses, reluctantly breaking the kiss and stepping from Dusty's taut arms. She drew in gulps of cold air, calming her racing heart. Why on earth had she thrown herself at this man? Why did he make her so crazy?

Because she found herself wanting only one man in her life. Dusty.

A rueful smile tugged at his lips as he reached over to pluck strands of hay from her hair, his fingers lingering. He brushed the rim of her ear, eliciting shivers with his touch.

She couldn't let him do this. She couldn't entertain the notion that they had a future together. Not when she'd made her decision to leave town.

She gently pulled her hand from his and curled her hair behind her tingling ear. "I'm fine, for now. But this knocking me to the ground is turning into a pattern with you."

He grinned. "Hey, I was only protecting a pretty woman."

Her face grew warm at his compliment, but she knew she had to stop things right now. She smiled to soften the edge of her words. "Don't do it again."

"Yes, ma'am."

"We'd better get moving. Gran will be looking for her delivery. She has high expectations of us."

Dusty kept his eyes focused on the paved road before him, trying to block out the warm, attractive woman seated beside him. He really hadn't meant to push her down, although he doubted that Marilyn believed him. It reminded him of the first time they'd met in the rain. She'd slipped in a puddle because of him. He shook his head. He'd never been this clumsy before. And especially not around a woman.

Not any woman. Marilyn.

He guessed it was on par with the rest of the events in his life. Couldn't write. Didn't want to produce music. Losing focus in everything, except Marilyn. Who was leaving town.

He didn't want to think about that.

And then there was Marilyn's family. And this small town he'd come to like far too much. His mind argued with his heart like a dissonant chord: If you fall for this woman, this place, how are you ever gonna move on? Dusty suspected that his inner arguments weren't worth a whole lot. So far his heart hadn't heard a word his mind was saying.

His hands tightened on the steering wheel. Those thoughts sounded like the lyrics to a song. And it hit too close to home for comfort. Still, he tucked the words away in the back of his mind in the event he needed them in the future.

Even so, he had to admit that he hadn't tried very hard to pursue his music. Except for that one night he sat at the piano with the deep recesses of the night shrouding him, he hadn't tried. He hadn't touched the ivory piano keys that night, afraid just touching the instrument would somehow confirm his worst fears. That he'd lost his talent. He didn't want to contemplate the future without the creativity that defined him as a person.

"If you drive any slower, the sheriff will wonder what you're up to and stop us. Try explaining to my grandmother that you got a ticket by driving *under* the speed limit."

Dusty shot Marilyn a quick look. "I don't need that negative attention. It'll kill the mystery man image I've got going."

"Mystery man?"

"Yeah, you know. Guy shows up out of nowhere."

"Tennessee."

"Takes a room at the local boarding house."

"My grandmother's house is hardly a local place to stay."

"And works his way into the heart of the townspeople."

"You forgot to say unsuspecting townspeople. Which would imply you're up to something. Should I have a background check done on you?"

"No," he chuckled, vastly preferring this wordplay with Marilyn to his dismal thoughts about the future.

"You really like it here, don't you?"

Dusty heard the surprise in Marilyn's voice and grinned. Since she'd grown up here, she didn't see how a small town like Paineville could get under your skin and make you want to stick around. Plant roots. Raise a bunch of kids. "Yeah. It grows on you."

"I just don't get it. I've been trying to leave for years."

"I hate to say this, but you haven't been very successful."

"I guess I'm the female equivalent of George Bailey from *It's a Wonderful Life*."

"Until this Charlotte move. You sure you're okay about that decision?"

After a protracted silence, Dusty glanced over to find Marilyn pensively staring out the window. Her frown made him wonder what she was thinking. Or if she might be changing her mind. "Do you have an answer for that question?"

"I'm working on it."

"Okay, skip that. What would make you want to stay?"

"I don't think I should answer that."

"So you've thought about staying?" His chest tightened, waiting for her response.

"I'm not saying yes."

"But you're not saying no."

"Why does what I do matter to you?"

He thought for a few minutes, careful to say the right words. "I like you, Marilyn. I like your family, this town."

"And . . ."

And what?

"Hey, you missed the turnoff." She leaned forward and braced her hand on the dashboard, turning to look out the window.

Dusty slammed on the brake pedal, then switched gears and did a three-point turn. "Guess I can't do two things at one time."

Marilyn laughed, her dulcet tone washing over him as she slid close and he pivoted the vehicle around. Her shoulder pressed into him and he did everything within his power not to wrap a protective arm around her. There had been way too much touching today, and he didn't think he could play the part of a gentleman much longer.

The scent of her floral fragrance mixed with hay filled his head with her close proximity. Man, she was driving him crazy. All he wanted to do was grab her and kiss her again. Talk about well and truly losing it.

He backed in close to the edge of the cordoned-off fairgrounds, jumping out to lower the tailgate and unload the hay. A few guys he'd met since coming to town were nearby, so he called on them to help.

"I can do this," Marilyn huffed.

"I'm sure you can, but these guys promised to help." Two men approached to the truck. "Right guys?"

One glanced at the other and shrugged his shoulders. "Sure, whatever."

Marilyn planted her elbow on the rim of the truck bed. "Oh, that was convincing."

"Look, with the way you've been falling when I'm around, I don't want to take any chances."

Her eyes opened wide. "Falling? Around you?"

"Well, you have been."

"Because you've somehow caused it to happen."

"Right. Like I came to town looking for an unsuspecting woman to fall at my feet every time I turn around."

A voice sounded behind them. "It'll take one heck of a guy to get my sister to fall for you."

Dusty swung around to face Ty Banner.

"I'm not falling for anyone. I'm leaving, remember?" Marilyn turned on her heel and stomped away.

Dusty exhaled a disgusted sigh. "I certainly impressed her."

Ty slapped him on the shoulder. "Don't take it personal. Marilyn's bristly around most men. Though I have to admit she hasn't minded running around town with you."

Dusty remained silent, waiting to hear the brotherly admonition or man-to-man advice.

"My grandmother is still conniving to get you two together."

"I know. She hasn't exactly been sneaky about it."

"Want the long or short of it?"

"Do I have a choice?"

Ty chuckled. "It hasn't been easy for Marilyn, growing up in a town that has a long-term memory. My mother made things hard for us before she took off, and I'm afraid my sister has really felt the brunt of that. She really won't date much."

"She's special. There's no need for her to hide."

"But she does. Look, man, she's different with you. More confident. Just give her a chance."

"I'm not the one who's leaving."

"Play your cards right, and she won't either."

Ty sauntered off, leaving Dusty to consider his words. He didn't figure Marilyn as the type to give up her ambitions just for some guy who blew into town. Then again, maybe he was selling himself short. Once he had his writing ability back, he'd show her he could make a future.

If, that is.

You have to try, his inner voice urged him. He stared at the crowd, straining to catch a glimpse of Marilyn. She was out of his line of sight, yet he felt her presence as surely as if she were standing right beside him. Smelled the traces of her perfume. In a short time, she'd come to mean more to him than he imagined possible.

He wanted a future, a future that included her. Them. Together.

And maybe, with her by his side, his writing ability would return.

"What are you going to do about this?" one of the workers called to him, pointing to the hay. Dusty shook his head, stunned by the revelation that had just struck him, and turned to help the worker haul the last few bales of hay from the truck. What was he going to do about the situation with Marilyn?

"Let's get it over by the band stage."

Dusty joined the men hauling the bales, glad he'd stayed in shape all these years. He brushed stray bits of hay from his shirt and blue jeans, his hand stopping mid-air as the band tuned up on stage. Dixie Highway.

His gaze moved slowly to take in the scene, a flicker of something—envy?—biting his chest. The pianist ran his fingers deftly up and down the keyboard. The guitarist plucked a few notes to find the right key, then broke into a familiar lick. The leader nodded, and on the downbeat, they united in an impromptu version of . . . the first hit Dusty had ever written.

He stood, rooted to the spot, the wave of music crashing over his head. Memories of when he penned the lyrics careened into his mind and gut, bringing with them the remembrance of a time when he'd been young and focused and ready to take the music world by storm.

He'd driven to his grandmother's house after his late shift at a local manufacturing plant. As he drove, lyrics came into his mind. On impulse, he pulled a napkin and pen from the glove box, almost hitting a tree in the process, and began to scribble the words as he steered. By the time he made it safely into the driveway, the melody played in his mind. He sat in the cab of his truck for so long, Grandma brought out a sandwich and soda.

Now, these guys hit all the subtle notes of the song, nailing the sound just as professional studio musicians would do. As he might do.

They finished the catchy tune with a rousing crescendo and launched into another song. Dusty didn't recognize the lyrics and guessed it must be one of their original songs. Instead of sounding like a novice group, these guys got tighter the longer they played.

When he'd heard them the other night, he'd been more distracted by Marilyn than the music. All he'd thought about was how he wanted to kiss her sweet lips. Now, in this outside venue, the band shone with talent. Dusty couldn't believe he'd missed it.

From behind him, hands clapped in time with the rhythm. Some of the locals sang along.

He knew Dixie Highway was good, but now he recognized their true talent. In his experience, he knew they were good enough to make it big. In radio format, they'd wow their listening audience. And Dusty had no doubt he could bring them into the studio and produce a dynamite debut album. Which meant lots of hours in the studio. Big money and fame.

And the rat race he'd only just escaped.

He swung around and headed to his truck, desperately needing to make tracks away from here. The music made him face the fact that he'd lost the dream. He'd gotten sidetracked and wanted to make big money, at the expense of who he really was. A man would live by his words. Only now the words wouldn't come. He'd paid a big price for success and found he didn't like himself very much for selling out.

He paused only for seconds when he caught sight of Marilyn enjoying the music. A big smile graced her

Tara Randel

lips, her eyes were sparkling with joy, and her skin glowed from spending the afternoon outdoors. She noticed Dusty standing there and she brightened even more.

The fact that he and Marilyn were so in tune pleased him most of the time. But right now, this personal crisis was more than he could handle. He had to resolve it one way or another.

As the last note of the tune faded in the airwaves around him, Dusty stalked to his truck, breathing deeply. Raw adrenaline threatened to undermine his steely determination. He would not go back to producing for a record company. Even if he never wrote another word to a song.

Chapter Eight

Marilyn watched as Dusty drove away, concern wrinkling her forehead. Where was he off to in such a rush? Her grandmother hadn't been near him, so she didn't think he was off on another errand. One minute he'd been enjoying the band, the next minute the music seemed to trouble him.

And then it hit her.

He had that trapped look on his face, the same one she'd seen many times when she looked in the mirror. Was Dixie Highway a reminder of his past life? Or was he worried about his inability to compose music? Or a combination of the two?

Should she go talk to him? Maybe he'd rather be alone. The uncertainty of what to do set her aback. She usually knew how to handle people and situations—it came with her job. Of course, she'd never in her life came across a man like Dusty. Still, her indecision weighed heavily.

"Marilyn. I'm surprised to see you here mingling with the volunteers."

Marilyn closed her eyes briefly and took a deep breath. Kitty. Why was she always turning up at the oddest of times? "I'm helping out today."

"Usually you're holed up in the office. Could that handsome boarder of yours be the reason you're out and about?" Kitty pointed to the truck rumbling off in the distance.

"My grandmother needed help, so Dusty and I have been working together," she said, trying to control her anxiety as she watched the brake lights on the pickup disappear around a corner.

"All alone? Just the two of you?"

Marilyn groaned inwardly. Why Kitty? Why now? "Did you want something?"

"Just curious."

"Look, if you want to know something, just ask me."

Kitty's perfectly manicured hand flew to cover her neck. A large diamond sparkled in the last rays of the setting sun. "Really. I wouldn't be that crass."

"Unlike me, you mean?" Marilyn couldn't help but notice Kitty's trendy sweater over pressed designer jeans and highly polished boots. Unlike her own sweatshirt and worn jeans and the bits of hay sticking out of her hair.

As Marilyn ran her fingers through her hair, she caught Kitty's wide-eyed surprise at the short, non-manicured nails. Marilyn didn't try to hide them, like she might have in the past.

Kitty's gaze met hers. "I didn't say that, either. My, you're in a mood." She smoothed her pants and continued talking. "I know we haven't gotten along in the past, but surely now that we're adults, that could change."

Marilyn knew when Kitty wanted information, especially when she feigned concern. "So just ask."

"Alright." She paused and pursed her painted lips. "Are you and Dusty an item?"

Marilyn almost wanted to laugh. An item? She'd made more than sure that they were no such thing. "We're friends."

"So you don't mind if he were to date another woman?"

"Any idea who this woman would be?" she asked innocently, hiding unfounded jealousy with a cool, unflappable exterior.

"I don't know for certain. But I do know he'd make a fine Harvest King."

"To your queen?"

"I can't help it if I win the crown often." Kitty pouted. "People just vote for me. I mean, except for last year, I've pretty much had the queen position sewn up." She paused for a minute, her heavily made-up eyes troubled. "It's what I do, Marilyn."

"I guess the other ladies in town just don't lobby hard enough for that honor."

A shadow passed over Kitty's face and Marilyn ignored a sharp twing of conscience. Why did she let Kitty bring out her less-than-stellar side?

"It's just that Dusty's been so friendly to everyone he's met. Why, the town council thinks the world of him."

The town council? When on earth had Dusty met with them? It puzzled her why he showed so much interest in this town. He probably knew as many people as she did, and she'd lived here all her life.

"What has he done to win such high esteem?"

"He's thrown himself right into the spirit of the harvest festival." Kitty beamed, her eyes bright. "This town has always prided itself on the strength of its volunteers. Other towns in the county are nowhere near as civic-minded as we are."

That was true, and Dusty had certainly gotten involved. In the short time since he'd arrived, he endeared himself to this town. The sting of envy pinched Marilyn. She'd been born and raised here and didn't have as many friends as Dusty did. He seemed to be years ahead of her when it came to belonging. How did he do it when she struggled? What was she missing?

"And you know how important this annual event is to the scholarship fund," Kitty continued, drawing Marilyn back into the dreaded conversation. Kitty's husband had been a big proponent of the scholarship, and Kitty had followed in his cause after his death.

Marilyn knew all about the scholarship. Her brother, Ty, had been one of the first recipients of the fund. She'd qualified too, but instead of going to a state university she'd chosen to attend a local business school, which eventually led to getting her real estate license.

"Yes, the scholarship will mean a lot to a someone. And it looks like my grandmother has gone all out to make this festival very successful."

Kitty drew herself up. "Yes, she has helped."

"Helped? More like planned the entire thing."

"Different committees have worked together in the initial stages."

Marilyn bit the inside of her cheek. Debating her grandmother's role on the Festival committee with Kitty was futile. The woman would never acknowledge a member of the Banner household contributing to a worthy cause.

Kitty adjusted the purse strap on her shoulder. "Just wanted to stop and chat. I'm off to make my rounds."

"Have fun."

"Before I go, I want you to know that I really do take this festival seriously. I know I come across as the pretty face who wins the contests, but I've learned in the past year that life can throw you a tragedy you'd never expect." Kitty gazed at Marilyn, her wistful expression causing Marilyn to rethink her opinion of her.

"I'm sure you have."

"Enough of that. I'm off to see where I can help." Kitty wiggled her fingers. "Ta."

"Ta," Marilyn muttered under her breath before searching for Ty.

She found him at the center of the fairgrounds, industriously hammering planks of wood together. "What is that?"

"A platform," Ty answered.

"Gee, that's so obvious I never would have figured it out."

"Smart mouth."

"Really, what's the platform for?"

"Can't say."

"Says who?"

"Ruby Sue."

"Do you think for once you could consider calling her Gran? She *is* your grandmother."

"Nope. Tried it once. Didn't feel right." Ty resumed hammering.

She rolled her eyes.

"I just do as I'm told."

"Yeah, right."

"So did you come over here to bother me, or do you need something?" Ty stood upright and pulled a cloth from his back pocket to wipe the sweat from his brow.

"Actually, I need a ride home."

Ty's eyebrows rose. "Where's Dusty? I thought you were with him."

"I was. He took off a few minutes ago."

"Another errand?"

She shrugged. "Actually, I don't know. It was weird."

Ty laid down his hammer and frowned at Marilyn. "Do you think something is wrong?"

Marilyn had a hunch it had to do with his music dilemma, but didn't want to speculate about it to her brother. "Maybe he just forgot something he had to do. Gran keeps him pretty busy."

"Let me pack up and we'll leave. It's time to head home, anyway." He grabbed his tool box and tossed the tools inside.

"I'll find Gran. She really needs to get home and rest, especially with the Festival ready to start. She's been really good about delegating, but I'm still concerned about her health. She might overdo things."

Marilyn made her way past the busy volunteers and

began to worry until she found her grandmother seated with Mayor Paine, the two deep in discussion.

"Hi, Gran. Ty's ready to take us home."

"I'm more than ready. These old bones just ain't what they used to be."

"Nonsense, Ruby Sue." The mayor chuckled. "You'll outlive us all."

"Kind of you to say, Mayor. I just might prove you right."

The mayor let out a booming laugh while Ruby Sue walked beside Marilyn.

"Where's Dusty?" She looked around her, fully expecting him to join them.

"He left earlier."

Gran frowned. "What did you say to him?"

"Nothing. Why would you even say that?"

"Because you have a way of making gentlemen uncomfortable around you."

She stepped back, surprised by her grandmother's sobering words. Did she always do that? Maybe, but not with Dusty. She enjoyed being with him. The time they spent together left her longing for more of his electrifying touch. She waited with breathless anticipation for the heated kisses that sent her nerve endings haywire. She'd never felt that with another man.

"Not this time, Gran. He took off on his own accord."

"Hope nothin's wrong."

"I'll see what I can find out."

"I was hopin' you would," Ruby Sue said, hiding a smile.

The crescent sliver of the moon did little to illuminate Marilyn's path through the backyard. She approached the trailer warily, led by the single porch light. Suppose Dusty was inside but didn't want company? Especially after the way he took off from the fairgrounds. Alone. Marilyn knew there was nothing worse that imposing on another person who wanted to be left alone.

A flicker, then the steady light from the small kitchen brightened the window. Well, now she knew for sure he was home.

She climbed the rickety steps to the door and knocked, sticking her chilly hands deep into her coat pockets. The warmth of the day had quickly disappeared once the sun set.

The door swung open. Dusty stood silhouetted in the light flooding out around him. He'd changed into a gray sweater and black jeans, and stood there in his stocking feet.

"What're you doing?" she asked when he made no attempt to greet her.

"Minding my own business," he crabbed.

"Hmm. Sounds to me like your having a pity party."

He ran his hand over his face. "C'mon in."

She stepped over the threshold into the warmth of the trailer. The pungent scent of coffee lingered in the air. From the back of the trailer she could hear the faint strains of country music. "You sure left the fairgrounds in a hurry."

He pointed to the couch. "Have a seat."

After removing her jacket, she sat, perched on the edge of the cushion. Waiting.

"Want some coffee?"

"No. Just an explanation."

He took a seat in the chair opposite her and sighed. "Dixie Highway is good."

She sat back, perplexed. "That's why you took off? Because they sounded good?"

"You don't understand."

"Enlighten me."

Dusty rubbed his eyes with one hand before speaking. "Did you hear the first song they played?"

She nodded.

"I wrote it."

"Whoa! You wrote that song? I assumed you were good from your other hits, but I had no idea how good." She paused a minute, confused why he'd be downcast when he should be so proud. "Okay, so they did a good job today. And they played your hit. What has that got to do with you?"

"Part of me says I should help them out. Make a record at least."

"But you're out of the business."

"Marilyn, a band with that much natural talent doesn't just show up on your doorstep. I want to keep them from losing their unspoiled sound."

"So, call someone you know. If they're that good, anyone can produce them." She didn't want to see him slip back into the world that had caused him such heartache.

A slight smile pulled at his lips. "You definitely don't have the mindset of a producer."

"I'm just going by what you told me. Besides, there are other producers out there who would probably be more than happy to work with the band."

"I know." He leaned forward in the chair, rested his elbows on his knees and clasped his hands together.

"There's just something in me that sees talent and I want to highlight it. It's the creative part of me. Until the business aspect rears its head. Then I go into this alter ego." He leaned back into the chair and stared up at the ceiling. "That's why I took off earlier. I had to seriously think about how to find the balance in my life."

Marilyn sank deeper into the cushions. How on earth could she help him? She had no point of reference to understand his pain. Yet her heart urged her to try, to show that she cared. If she could get him to experience the joy of writing again, maybe he'd see his talent from a different perspective.

She sat up straight. "Dusty, how do you usually start to write a song?"

His eyebrows bunched and he stared at her as if she'd asked him to jump off the nearest cliff. "How do I start?"

"Yes. With a melody or the words?"

"It depends. Sometimes I'll be out somewhere and the lyrics pop into my mind, kinda like a poem. I write them down until I get a melody to go with it. Most times I hear the music first. Why?"

She licked her lips. "I was thinking that maybe we could write a song, you know, for fun."

"What?"

"As a . . . gift for my grandmother. She's put so much time and effort into the festival. I thought maybe—"

"We could write a song? Together?"

"Come on, it can't be that hard."

He scowled at her and her heart lifted. She definitely had his interest.

"Look, I know I don't have any experience in this, but I can help you come up with ideas. I've listened to country music and bluegrass my whole life. All we need is a pickup truck, a dog, and a pretty girl, and we're pretty much set."

He gaped at her. "You're kidding, right?"

She smiled. "Am I?"

He chuckled, but she could see him visibly relax. "I know what you're doing and I'm not biting."

"Dusty, I'm really not kidding, here. How do we get started?" She scooted to the edge of the cushion.

"Wait. You're serious?"

"Not about the truck and dog. But with the woman, yes. We've got Gran."

His eyes met hers and she could see him seriously consider her outrageous suggestion of writing a song out of the blue. Her audacity surprised even herself.

"I suppose I could come up with something."

"Just think about Gran's down home cooking as a reward."

Dusty leaned back deeply into the chair, steepling his fingers under his chin. A faraway look clouded his eyes. He remained silent for long moments before asking, "Are you thinking the piano or guitar?"

"Oh, I hadn't thought that far. Um, guitar?" she guessed.

"Yeah, that's what I thought too." He jumped up and headed to the back of the trailer. He returned with a custom-made leather guitar case, a pad of paper and a pencil. He removed the instrument, eyeing it as though he hadn't touched it in a long while.

"Fast tempo or more of a ballad?" He seemed to question himself more than her.

"We're talking Ruby Sue, here. Foot-stompin' please."

He nodded, his fingers positioned on the neck while his free hand picked the strings. After toying with a few different melodies, he surprised her by coming up with a sound that actually fit her grandmother. He paused to write down the chords, then continued.

Marilyn sat back, listened, and watched. The strain lines on Dusty's forehead disappeared as he lost himself in the music. This went on for so long, Marilyn lost track of the time. When he got to a place where he seemed satisfied, he put the guitar to the side and picked up the paper.

"Okay, let's work on the lyrics."

She feigned surprise. "You want me to help?"

"It was your idea."

"How do you usually decide what words to use?"

"I look for a hook. Something to grab the listener."

"I was thinking we could play up all her help in the community, how everyone loves her . . ."

"Okay, now we need specific details that get to the heart of the woman. That's what draws listeners in. Tell them an emotional story they can relate to and they're ours."

"Okay, you're the professional. Show me how it's done."

"Let's concentrate on the lady in question. What other parts of her life or personality do you want to focus on?"

"Gosh, I don't know."

"If you were writing about her life, what important things about her would you include?"

"Well. She's tough on those she loves, but she's

loyal. And she loves us, no matter how brusque she is. The townsfolk really admire her and she makes the best pies around." She stopped her list and grinned. "Can you work with that?"

"Yep. Instead of a truck I'll focus on her pies."

"And instead of a dog, include her cat."

"I think we have the makings for a little ditty here."

They bandied lyrics around, laughing at each other's suggestions. She tried to lead Dusty off on a tangent, only to be amazed at how he'd draw them back to the original idea. No doubt about it, this man was good.

Marilyn stifled a yawn, then glanced at her watch. It was after midnight.

"I need to get going. We've got a full day tomorrow."

Dusty walked her to the door, grabbing his coat from the wall hook and humming the tune they'd cooked up. "Thanks for tonight. It felt good to work on a song again, even if we were just horsing around."

"This wasn't just a lark, Dusty. It may not be any of my business, but I don't think you've lost your talent. You just need to keep your priorities in order. If the creative and business aspects of music have to intertwine for you, then learn to keep the business end at a minimum. Don't let it keep you from what you love most: creating."

His brow furrowed as he stared at her. "I've got to think about it. Maybe I can balance both the writing and the producing."

"You won't know until you try."

"Yeah." He leaned against the door jamb, shoving his hands into his jeans pockets. "I guess the same could be said for you," he volleyed back, effectively turning his problem away to focus on hers.

"Yes," she whispered. They both had to settle their lives. And that would mean going in opposite directions. Seems like she'd killed their chances to be together before they even got started.

Dusty shrugged into his coat while Marilyn turned the knob. They stepped into the cold air. For the first time this year she could see her breath as white puffs in the porch light.

The night smelled earthy, of dank ground and decaying leaves. The stars glittered in the vast sky, winking with promise. Marilyn concentrated on the path before her, keeping her mind from dwelling on Dusty.

"Thanks for walking me home," she said when they reached Ruby Sue's porch.

Dusty reached out and brushed her cheek with his fingers. "Thanks for caring about my problem."

"Hey, that's me. I earned the helper badge in Girl Scouts."

He grinned. "Really, I mean it."

He leaned to brush his lips over hers. His warm breath fanned her cheek and she stepped into his embrace, snuggling close. The kiss moved from teasing to bold in a matter of moments. Marilyn lost herself to the pleasure, forgetting that they didn't have a future together. If she repeatedly told herself she didn't care, maybe she'd believe it. And for now, she'd revel in Dusty alone.

"Marilyn," he breathed against her lips.

"Don't." She saw the desire in his eyes and knew it was for a moment. Not a lifetime.

"Stay here," he whispered against her lips, his breath warm.

She ignored the warmth in her heart as she moved out of his embrace, forging a much-needed distance between them. "I'll see you tomorrow."

She rushed up the steps and through the front door into the safety of the house. Wishing just once that she could be like her mother and take what she wanted for a short time, no matter the cost.

For the first time in her life it became glaringly evident that she wasn't anything like her mother.

She wanted happily ever after. With one man. With Dusty.

Unfortunately, her decision to leave Paineville ruined any chance of that happening.

Chapter Nine

"**I** don't believe this. Arlette canceled my appointment again. I wanted her to touch up my hair color." Marilyn replaced the phone into the cradle and sank into a high-back kitchen chair.

"Don't see why you scheduled an appointment today, what with the festival startin'."

"I just wanted to look nice."

Her brother, Gabe, strolled into the kitchen and kissed her lightly on the head. "You always look nice. You shouldn't tamper with perfection."

"Ugh."

Gabe chuckled.

"Well, he's right. Don't know why you have to be a blond."

"Haven't you heard? They have more fun."

"Guess you'll just have to do without."

"I can always wear a hat."

Ruby Sue harumphed and left the room.

"It's only the festival. Its not like you're trying to

128

impress a customer." Gabe leaned his hip against the counter, ready for the day dressed in jeans and a bulky sweater.

Marilyn frowned. True, she wasn't working. But she wanted to look good. For Dusty. "Besides, I could always win festival queen this year."

"Of course you could," Gabe agreed, but she didn't miss the surprised lift of his eyebrows.

Don't hold your breath.

She'd never told her family that she wanted to win just once. Seeing the compassion in their eyes when she lost would have been more than she could bear.

Marilyn expelled a long sigh. No doubt Kitty would win again. Marilyn had just been prickly when she teased about Kitty lobbying for the role, but she had to admit, the woman always won. And deep inside, Marilyn had a sneaking suspicion that Dusty would be crowned king. Not that he'd like it, but he'd be nice about it. Then he'd be paired up with Kitty.

She clenched her jaw, forcing herself not to think about the possibility.

"I'm sure Dusty thinks you're gorgeous," Gabe teased. "We all do."

"You have to think that way. You're family."

"Seriously, you don't give yourself enough credit."

"And neither do you. You've been moping around the house ever since you got home. What's up with you?"

Gabe poured the last of the coffee into his mug and took a seat across the table from her. "Emily was having behavioral problems at her old school."

"How bad?"

"Bad enough to get an in-school suspension."

"What's her explanation?"

"She doesn't have one. She started hanging around a couple of girls that seem to be troublemakers. The light finally dawned, and that's when I decided she needs to be around family."

"She seems fine to me. Think you nipped this phase in the bud?"

"I won't know till she settles in here. Time will tell."

Marilyn hesitated a millisecond before asking her next question. "What's really going on with you? Just you."

"I've been . . . restless. I don't enjoy being a lawyer anymore. I used to love preparing my cases," he shot her a rueful grin, "and winning. But the last case I handled . . ." He stopped and shook his head. "It hit too close to home."

"In what way?"

"A young woman went into a coma with no signs of gaining consciousness. Her husband received some money from the insurance company, then he wanted to turn off the respirator. Her parents fought to keep her alive, so we spent months going back and forth to court, never getting anywhere."

"Is she still alive?"

"Just before I resigned, I heard that the final verdict had come in for the husband. Since the parents are going to lose their daughter, they're suing him for some of the insurance money. It's a total mess. And as a human being, the whole case disgusted me."

Marilyn didn't doubt that. Gabe had been passionate about practicing law, but his love for his wife had gone much deeper. Her death had pierced him to the bone. That would affect his handling of the case.

"You still miss Cindy."

"Every day." Gabe took a deep breath. "Since she's not here, I have to do the best I can with Emily. I figured if Gran could keep the three of us in line, Emily didn't stand a chance."

Marilyn smiled. "Emily loves Gran. And you. Maybe she's acting out because she misses Cindy and doesn't know how else to express herself."

"When Mom left you didn't act up."

"True. But deep down I knew she was out there somewhere, alive. Emily doesn't have that."

He nodded. "She needs a woman's influence in her life. Now she'll get it."

"Ever think about dating again?"

A shadow passed over his face. "Sometimes. But I have to say, I feel disloyal to Cindy."

"She'd want you to go on. You know that, don't you?"

"In my head, yeah. Not so much in my heart."

"You're home now. Maybe you'll meet a nice girl who won't mind an instant family and you'll fall in love."

"I'm not holding my breath."

"It could happen."

Gabe stared down into his cup, obviously not convinced. Marilyn breathed a silent prayer for her brother, then rose to finish cleaning up the breakfast dishes.

"C'mon, y'all," Ruby Sue hollered from the recesses of the house. "Ten minutes and we've got to leave.

Oh, and Marilyn, run down to the trailer and holler for Dusty. I didn't see him drive by this morning."

"Pushy," Marilyn muttered under her breath, secretly thrilled at any reason to call on Dusty.

Gabe brought his cup to the sink. "Time to get started."

"That's what I'm afraid of." She ran upstairs to change into black corduroy slacks, a warm multicolored sweater, and hiking boots. She stopped in front of the mirror, ignored the hint of natural brunette beginning to show in her hair, and made the decision to leave it loose around her shoulders. She added gold earrings and added a splash of perfume before dashing down the stairs to do her duty.

The brisk air invigorated her as she jogged down the path toward the trailer. It wasn't so hard to see the old homestead, as it were, knowing that Dusty resided inside.

She ran up the steps and pounded on the front door. And waited. The wooden porch creaked as she danced from one foot to the other, blowing warm air on chilled fingers.

When he didn't respond, she pounded harder and longer.

Concern took precedent over the chills. "Dusty? Open up, it's Marilyn." She tried to peek in the kitchen window but curtains obscured her view.

"Hey, are you alright in there?"

She lifted her hand to knock again when the door jerked open. Dusty stood on the other side, dressed only in a pair of faded denim jeans, his sleepy, hooded eyes squinting in the bright light of day.

"Thank goodness," Marilyn breathed. She took a

step forward, her mouth suddenly dry at the sight of him. His broad shoulders filled the doorway. Dark, curly hair covered the defined muscles of his torso. She'd tried to imagine what he'd look like without wearing a shirt, but the real thing rendered her speechless.

"C'mon in." He ran a hand through his tousled hair, oblivious to her heated flush. "What time is it?"

"Just after ten o'clock," she managed to croak out.

He scratched at the shadow along his jaw. "Jeez, I overslept. I never do that."

"Late night?"

"Yeah," he muttered, realizing he was only half dressed. "I'll be right back."

Marilyn sighed. She'd been enjoying the view.

He returned minutes later, buttoning a dark denim shirt over a black T-shirt. He sat at the end of the couch to lace up his work boots. "Your grandmother will be upset if I mess up her schedule."

Marilyn waved her hand. "She just wanted to make sure you were okay. Don't worry about any errands, she sent Gabe."

He leaned back against the cushion and closed his eyes. "I need coffee."

"I'll get it. You look beat." She shrugged off her jacket and headed to the neat-as-a-pin kitchen. She found the coffee and filters in no time and scooped the grounds into the maker. "Care to explain the late night?"

Dusty sat forward, his hands resting on his knees, rubbing the fabric over his legs. "After you left last night I called my soon-to-be ex-partner in Nashville."

Surprise rocked her. "Really? After midnight? I thought you were finished with him."

"I was. Even though I still have the legalities to deal with." He waved that train of thought away. "The point is, when you took me to hear Dixie Highway I connected with them. I recognized the hunger, the love of the music, in their eyes. I realized I've been missing that."

Marilyn sank down on the couch next to him. "So what did you do?

"After I got off the phone I went down to the Saucy Sow and caught the last set. I spent the remainder of the night, or should I say morning, with them. We talked about their future, where they want to be in their career. I even jammed with them for a while."

"Did it make you homesick?"

"Some. But we made some definite decisions about their future."

"A future that features the band?"

"And coffee." Dusty stood and strode into the kitchen.

Marilyn started down at her neatly trimmed fingernails. Did she dare question him more about his plans? Did she want to know?

"Man, it felt good to work with raw talent again," Dusty told her as he walked back into the room. "Anyway, I was up till almost dawn. That explains my tardiness this morning."

"As long as it doesn't happen again," she teased. Besides, she didn't think he could look any better. He had that relaxed, sleepy expression of a person not in too much of a hurry, regardless of the fact that Ruby Sue was waiting for them.

He smiled at her before sipping his coffee. Her heart did a funny flipping thing in her chest. Would she want to start every day like this? Deep down she didn't want to analyze herself too closely. Her answer might interfere with her plans.

"We should probably get going," she urged, wanting to escape her wayward thoughts.

"Right, let me get my coat."

She pulled on her jacket and waited by him by the door. He came back, mug in one hand, keys in the other. "Lead on."

They got into the truck and headed down the bumpy driveway. "I wouldn't be surprised if Matt shows up today."

"Matt?"

"My partner from Nashville."

"To try to talk you into coming back?"

He chuckled. "Of course. Businesswise, I can't do much for Dixie Highway right now, but I still have contacts who can work with them in the studio."

"So, would you be involved with any deal they made?"

"Maybe in the future."

Marilyn went still. This was the first time Dusty had mentioned the future in a positive tone since he arrived in town. Maybe things were finally becoming clear in his life. Good for him. Bad for her. Now that she'd made a sure decision, her life plans suddenly seemed clear as mud.

Once they arrived at the fairgrounds, Ruby Sue set them to work. Marilyn didn't see much of Dusty after that. Craft and homemade food booths were set up along one end of the park. The pony ring would be at the south end, the band stage at the north. All the volunteers had their jobs mapped out for them and they scurried to their assigned areas.

"Did you see what your brother's done?" Casey sidled up beside Marilyn at a crafts booth she would oversee.

"Judging from your tone, it can't be good."

"He built a platform, complete with matching thrones, for the king and queen of the festival. Can you believe that? He swore he'd never participate in what he calls, and I quote, 'a hokey tradition.' "

Marilyn grinned. "Since becoming happily married he's done a lot of things he said he'd never do."

"He just better not participate in any other way, or he'll be sleeping in the barn."

Marilyn pictured her brother relegated to the barn, sleeping among the inventory for Casey's craft catalog. That would last about ten minutes, tops, before Casey would be joining him.

"I'm sure he's not one of the candidates. They usually get singles for that."

Casey didn't look relieved. "He doesn't have to look so smug."

"Casey, if I know my brother, he's got some poor sucker lined up for king duty."

"That's what worries me."

Casey's cousin, Bonnie, the queen of gossip, rushed into the booth area, her red hair bouncing around her flushed face. "Did you hear? Rumor has it that Kitty is gonna make harvest queen again."

Marilyn rolled her eyes. "There's a newsflash."

"Well, she's all excited because that new guy in town, Dusty, is rumored to be king."

Marilyn's stomach dropped and her throat tightened. She suspected this would happen, but the reality stung worse than she'd thought.

"We don't know anything until the mayor makes the announcement," Casey assured them. "For all we know the winner could be Buddy Lee."

Marilyn and Bonnie exchanged bemused glances.

"Look," Casey pointed out, "all I'm saying is that we shouldn't jump to conclusions."

"Why? What difference does it make if Dusty wins?" Bonnie asked. "He's a nice guy and good-looking to boot. Kitty could do worse."

"Bonnie, now isn't a good time . . ." Casey shot her a wary glance.

"Excuse me," Marilyn mumbled, working her way through the crowd to the public rest rooms. Of course the women in town would love to have Dusty win. It was no secret that he was as popular as he was handsome. A real fantasy come true.

Yet envy ate at Marilyn. Once again Kitty would win. Only this time Marilyn's heart had a stake in the outcome. Even if she refused to admit the reason why.

She finally reached the public rest room, more than ready for a minute of solitude. She slipped in through the door, group laugher momentarily dragging her out of her depressing thoughts before she fully entered.

"She'd never win. You don't have anything to worry about with Marilyn."

"I don't know." Kitty's worried voice followed. "Her grandmother is running things this year. And Marilyn has kept a pretty high profile, with her running around and helping this year. She stands a chance."

Surprised, Marilyn took a step back.

"She's not up to your caliber."

"Still," Kitty said, "her family is very popular. It might be that my time is over."

"Please," came another voice, dripping in cattiness. "All she's good for is selling houses to compensate for the fact that she can't find a man and make her own home. However you look at it, the apple doesn't fall far from the tree."

Marilyn gasped, turning away before she could hear Kitty's response. Heart pounding and tears burning her eyes, she caught sight of her grandmother and niece at the barrier surrounding the pony pen and ran to them.

Ruby Sue's forehead creased, her maternal instincts switching into full gear as Marilyn approached. "What's wrong, child?"

"Let's get away from the crowd." Marilyn led Ruby Sue and Emily to the fringes of the park, away from prying ears and eyes.

"What's got you so riled up?"

Marilyn took a deep breath, her voice shaking as she spoke. "I overheard some women in the rest room. They were talking about the harvest queen, and how I'd never make it. It's not that I care about being queen so much, it's more of what those women said. It's because of . . ." She couldn't say the words.

"Your mother," Ruby Sue finished. She took Marilyn's trembling hand and pulled her farther from the crowd. "You've got no call to feel like this. You've never done a thing like your mama."

Marilyn's shoulders slumped. "Maybe we're not so different. She'd go off with any man, even if only for a short while. I can't even have a decent relationship with one man because I'm afraid people will think I'm easy like Mama. Either way, folks think Banner women can't keep a man. And they're right."

"Marilyn, listen to me. I raised you younguns to be proud of who you are. Where you came from. You're all grown up now, all chosen your paths." She placed a slim arm around Emily and pulled her close. "Some of the decisions have been wonderful. But some decisions haven't been so great. Either way, I'm proud of you all.

"You've hidden behind your mama's legacy long enough. You have nothin' to be ashamed of. You're a successful woman. You're polite and pretty and everyone that knows you loves you. What more do you want? You've got to get out of the past, girl. You can't change preconceived notions. But you can keep living the best life you know how."

Marilyn brushed away the tears that had trailed down her cheeks. "I know you're right, Gran. Why is it so hard?"

"Because no matter what your mama did, she's still your mama and you love her. Cain't help that. It's only natural for a child."

"But you've always been like my mama, been a constant my entire life. I couldn't have asked for better. I feel like I betray you when I feel badly about her leaving."

"I know that. And I still love you."

Marilyn sniffled before hugging Ruby Sue. "I love you, Gran. More than you know."

"Then do me a favor. Go out there. Hold your head high. Don't listen to those gossips who are jealous of you. Why else would they behave like that? They're threatened by you. Look at all you've done. What have they got to call their own?"

Marilyn pulled back. She thought back to the times over the years when different people had said mean things about her mother and her family. "Jealous?"

"Of course."

Jealous? Threatened? Marilyn had never allowed herself to believe that. She couldn't imagine someone as put-together as Kitty being jealous of her. Marilyn had been too busy working on her own image to notice a thing like that. Could Gran be right?

Now that she was older, she recognized her accomplishments over the years. She'd done it all on her own. Suddenly, she saw things in a new light. It explained so much.

"Besides," Ruby Sue continued, "Dusty doesn't care a bit about your mama's reputation. If you don't give that fellow a chance, you're gonna miss out on a husband and home for yourself."

Marilyn blinked, aware of a tingling in her stomach at the mention of Dusty's name. She couldn't cave in to Gran's meddling. She had her life staked out and it didn't include a long-term relationship with Dusty. How could it when she'd cemented her resolve to leave this town with its narrow-minded memory and inability to forgive her mama's past?

No, she'd get through this crisis. Alone. Like she'd always done.

Dusty scanned the crowd for a glimpse of Marilyn. Concern weighed on his shoulders. He'd tried to approach her earlier, just as she emerged from the ladies' room. She didn't see him, but he followed as she made a beeline to Ruby Sue, his chest tight after catching a glimpse of the tears misting her eyes.

He'd almost gone after her, then stopped in his tracks. Whatever the problem, he couldn't help her. He wasn't part of the family, who had years of love and advice for Marilyn to fall back on. He blew out a frustrated breath. Besides, he seemed to think his presence in her life might be important to Marilyn. She'd never given him any proof positive in that direction.

His mood sunk deeper.

"You keep pacing that same patch of grass and you'll be up to your knees in no time. Then how are you gonna dance with my sister?" Ty grinned at him while he hammered the finishing touch on one of the elaborate throne seats set on the dias.

"Something's up with her."

Gabe stood beside Ty, giving his brother instructions he didn't need. "I saw her with Gran. Whatever it is, they'll work it out."

Dusty glanced across the fairgrounds again. "Just wish I could help."

"You are," Ty assured him. "It's my experience that you gotta be patient with women."

Gabe hooted with laughter. "Oh, that's rich. Coming from the guy who had a lousy track record before he married Casey."

"Hey, Casey's taught me a lot about life since we've been married. Since before we were married. So now I feel the need to pass that information on."

Gabe shook his head. "You've only been married six weeks."

Ty winked. "Yeah, but what a great six weeks it's been."

Dusty deliberately shut off the banter between the brothers. Envy invaded his heart when he heard Ty's words. He wanted to be happy like that. And more and more he realized he wanted that happiness with Marilyn.

When she came back into the festival grounds, he let out a slow breath. "I'll be back," he announced and took off toward her.

He tapped her on the shoulder. A shy smile spread over her lips when she turned to face him. Her eyes held a hint of red. Had she been crying? Just the thought of her suffering was like a kick to his gut.

"I thought you were helping my brothers?" She wiped residual moisture from her cheek.

"I was. Am." He jammed his hands into his jeans pockets to keep from reaching out and comforting her.

"Ty actually let you leave a job?" Her small laugh broke her pensive expression.

"He didn't have any say."

Her smiled brightened. "A man who stands up to my brother. I like that."

He relaxed at her teasing tone. Obviously the crisis had passed. He wasn't sure, exactly, what possessed him just then, but he moved closer, brought his hand up to her chin to tip it upward, wanting nothing more than to kiss her. In plain sight. Before her family and the world.

He stood his ground, just staring at her, wanting to keep her close. He could read the look in her eyes—she wanted that kiss. After long static moments, she brushed a lock of hair behind her ear and looked away.

That's when he noticed the small crowd of people around them. Including his partner, Matt, who watched them with a wide grin on his face.

"Hey, Dusty old buddy. See you still have a way with the ladies."

Dusty flinched at the sound of his partner's voice. *No, no, no, not now.* He slowly turned to see Matt Fowler's jovial face.

"You're here sooner than I expected."

Matt sauntered over to shake Dusty's hand. "Nobody's heard from you for months. Then you up and call the company. I figured this band has to be a big deal."

"They're good, Matt."

"I have no doubt about it. I'll listen, then you and I will sit down and talk. I'm willing to extend you an offer from the company that can't be refused."

Dusty's voice turned steely. "You'd be surprised at what I can refuse."

Marilyn shifted beside him. He sighed. Who said timing was everything? Man, his stunk lately.

"Marilyn, this is Matt Fowler."

Matt took her hand and winked, then turned his attention back to Dusty. "Look, buddy, I'll admit I let you down back in Nashville."

"You hung me out to dry, *buddy.*"

"Yeah, I did do that. But I want to make it up to you. The company wants you back, Dusty. And this time you've got free rein in the sound booth. No more worrying about money and pleasing the big guys. That's where I come in."

"That's where you were supposed to be last time."

"I know." Matt actually looked chagrined by his

past behavior. That meant he might really be serious in this turnabout.

"Matt, hold that thought. I need to talk to Marilyn, then we can listen to the band."

"No problem." Matt took a few steps away, but stayed within listening distance.

Dusty looked at Marilyn, his mouth going dry when he glimpsed her tight lips.

"The record company is serious about Dixie Highway if they sent Matt," Dusty explained. "Especially from my recommendation alone. I think they have a shot."

"But . . . ?"

"There's probably a catch."

She tilted her head and stared at him.

"They'll want me to be the producer."

Matt quit eavesdropping and cut in. "That's right. We need Dusty back in Nashville where he belongs. And I'm prepared to make that happen. My boss authorized me to offer Dusty anything he wants, that's how serious they are."

Marilyn never veered her serious gaze from Dusty's eyes. "How soon?"

"As of yesterday," Matt answered.

Regret, and something deeper, more painful, played over her lovely face before she nodded and looked at Dusty. "Then I guess you found what you were looking for when you came here." She shot a glance at Matt. "You go on, Dusty. This doesn't involve me."

Dusty reached out to clasp her wrist, holding it tightly as he pierced his gaze with hers. "Yes, it does.

More than you know. More than either one of us has been willing to admit."

"You've been feeling it too?" Marilyn asked, surprise lighting her eyes.

He ran his thumb over her sensitive palm. "For quite some time."

A slight frown wrinkled her forehead. She took a deep breath. "There really seems to be more going on between us than I thought."

"I agree."

She met his gaze. "We're going to have to sit down and talk about this."

He nodded in hopeful expectation. "Later?"

But his hope plummeted when he heard the resignation in her voice. "Yes, later."

He watched her determined gait as she walked away, wondering what just happened to his life. When he woke up this morning he thought he may be on his way to having his future mapped out. Hoped he could talk Marilyn into that plan. But Matt's presence brought a new set of problems. Ones he swore he'd never find himself involved in again.

With blinding clarity, Dusty realized he'd fallen in love with a woman who wouldn't want to settle down with a man who had no direction, no clear grasp on his future. Would taking Matt's offer change that? At least he'd have something concrete to offer her.

But she'd already taken the job offer in Charlotte. A job that meant a lot to her. And he'd be off in Nashville. Would a long distance romance work? He'd seen it only rarely in the music world. Long hours in the studio, stress from the business, the combination of both usually hitting a breaking point. Besides, did he even want to leave Marilyn long enough to get re-established?

He blew out a frustrated breath. No, he didn't want to leave her. Ever.

Chapter Ten

Marilyn walked back toward the crafts booth, her back stiff. What difference did it make that Dusty might go back to his own world? She had no doubt that he'd take care of Dixie Highway. And she knew in her heart that he'd get his writing ability back. The evening she spent with Dusty working on a song proved it.

But producing meant he'd be going back to Nashville. That he'd leave, for good.

She shook her head, told herself she didn't care. What difference did it make? She was going to Charlotte. To start a new life. To head out on her own and see what would happen.

So why did her heart ache at the thought of Dusty leaving Paineville? She no longer had to worry about him as a boarder now that Gabe was home. And if he left? She'd been expecting it from the start. But at the start, her heart wasn't involved. Now she was afraid she'd fallen in love.

"Marilyn. Hold up."

She stopped and closed her eyes. Kitty. Not now.

Kitty skidded to a stop next to her. She was clearly out of breath and her cheeks were flushed. "That guy with Dusty, he's a music producer, right?"

"How could you possibly know that already?"

"He mentioned it to the mayor while he was searching for Dusty."

"That explains it." If you wanted to keep a secret, you didn't breath a word of it to Mayor Paine.

"Anyway, is it true? Are they going to make Dixie Highway an offer?"

"I wouldn't jump to conclusions. Dusty thinks they're good, but this other guy needs to hear them too."

Kitty craned her neck to look over the crowd. "Who is he?"

"Matt Fowler."

"Think he'll be around long?"

Marilyn stepped back to gauge Kitty's flushed face. "What are you up to?"

Kitty blinked. "Nothing. Nothing at all. Just curious is all." She angled her head in an innocent way that indicated she was scheming big time. "Is my hair all right?"

Marilyn frowned at the change in subject. "You're asking me?"

"Sure. Why wouldn't I? You always look stylish, even though you should go back to your natural hair color. Blond washes your skin tone out."

"Gee, thanks. I think."

"Maybe sometime we could go shopping together. Drive down to Atlanta and do some big-time mall hopping. Or spend a day of pampering." She covered her mouth with her hand, angling so only Marilyn could hear. "I think you need someone other than Arlette doing your hair."

Marilyn threw up her hands. "Okay. Wait. Hold on. Where's the Kitty I've always known, the woman who one-ups me all the time?"

"Why, Marilyn, if you weren't on to me, I'd be hurt."

"So explain."

Kitty shifted, clearly uneasy with her confession. "I've been thinking about things. How we've always been at odds. I think we should try to be friends."

Surprise rendered Marilyn speechless. For the first time in their lives, Kitty actually seemed sincere in what she said.

In his trademark booming voice, Mayor Paine announced on the bullhorn that the results were in for the King and Queen of the Festival.

"Oh," Kitty squealed. "I have to run. Can't keep my fans waiting." She hurried off to her group of friends who fussed over her and chattered away.

"What just happened?" Marilyn wondered out loud. So many changes were taking place lately, she didn't know how to react to it all.

Reluctantly, Marilyn joined the group that had gathered around the throne platform. Mayor Paine huffed as he climbed into prime position.

"Welcome one and all to the Paineville Harvest Festival. As you know, this is one of the big events for our town. Thanks to Ruby Sue Callahan." He nodded in her direction. After an uproaring of applause, he continued.

"Thanks to Ruby Sue, her festival committee, and countless volunteers, the Festival is a success. Already the donations we've brought in this year have surpassed last year's total."

Applause broke out again.

"For you folks visiting, please stop by the crafts booths to bring yourself home a reminder of the fair. And don't forget to check out the pies and other food our fine womenfolk have prepared.

"Before we get started, I have a surprise for Ruby Sue. Please give your attention to Dusty Haywood, a newly adopted Painevillite."

Directly across from the mayor, Dusty stepped up to the microphone on the band stage. A surge of pride welled in Marilyn as she watched him. His handsome face and confident stance assured that all eyes turned to him. "Thanks, folks. Even though I haven't been here long, Paineville has become home to me. Most of you know I'm involved in the music industry and I've been known to write a few songs."

"Only *Billboard* hits," someone shouted out.

Dusty chuckled. "Well, today, in honor of a town citizen who has done more than her fair share to make this festival a success, I've penned a new song. Hopefully another hit. But I didn't write the words by myself. Marilyn Banner gets credit for this too."

Marilyn smiled through the tears in her eyes while the crowd whooped and clapped. She could see Dusty through a blur, but he still looked wonderful to her.

"I've asked the band to play this song for all of you. In honor of Ruby Sue."

He stepped away from the mic as the lead singer came forward. "One and a two and a . . ." The band launched into a rowdy, foot-stomper that would make any relative of Ruby Sue's proud.

"So, what do you think?" Dusty asked as he came up behind Marilyn and dropped his arm over her shoulder.

"Now I know you're too good to be true."

"Hey, she deserves a moment of glory."

The music swelled in a rousing crescendo, so Marilyn stood on her toes to whisper in Dusty's ear. "Thank you."

He gazed at her, an enigmatic look on his face. "No, thank you."

She stood with Dusty's arm around her, his warmth surrounding and infusing her, imagining them as a couple. She rested her head on his shoulder and sighed dreamily when Dusty squeezed her in response. She could certainly get used to this.

There isn't another like her,
After her they broke the mold,
If you're looking for a place to belong,
Then Ruby Sue is home.

All too soon the song ended.

"Well folks, I do believe Mr. Haywood just put Paineville on the music map." Mayor Paine waited for the commotion to die down. "Ruby Sue, anything you want to say?"

The older woman waved him off, busy holding a hanky over her nose.

"I think that's the first time anyone has left my grandmother speechless." Ty's amused drawl sent renewed laughter through the crowd.

"Well, then," the mayor continued, "let's get on with the festivities." Hoots and claps echoed through the crowd as he held up the envelope clutched in his hand, waving it over his head. "Now, to the event we've all been waiting for. As far back as I can re- member, we've had a Harvest King and Queen to commemorate the day. Why, I, myself, had the honor of being king many years ago. Until I was paired up with the lovely queen who became my wife."

More clapping carried up to the stage.

"So now, we continue with tradition. The votes are in. Here in my hand I hold the results. Boys," he shouted over to the band. "Give me a drum roll."

Marilyn found herself holding her breath as the mayor ceremoniously opened the envelope with the slips of paper naming the winners inside. Each year she hoped to hear her name called out, and each year disappointment hit hard.

The mayor pulled out the first slip of paper. A huge grin spread across his jowls. "Ladies and gentlemen, let's welcome our new king. None other than Dusty Haywood."

"What? Oh, great," he muttered.

"Go on," Marilyn urged. "Enjoy it." She pushed him off so he stumbled into the crowd. People patted him on the back and congratulated him as he moved toward the makeshift dais.

He jumped up and shook hands with the mayor, then waved to the crowd. Marilyn laughed out loud at the surprised but pleased look on Dusty's handsome face. He might grumble, but he clearly reveled in the honor.

The mayor grabbed Dusty's hand to give him a

hearty shake. "You're one of us now, son. As mayor, I hereby pass on the king's crown to you." He balanced the crown on Dusty's head while Dusty made humorous comments and took it all in stride.

"Watch out, it may not come off," Ty yelled from the sidelines.

"Can I get last year's Queen, Miss Etta Sharp, to c'mon up here?" the mayor asked.

Etta, twenty-five and a local schoolteacher, shyly walked to the platform. On her head she sported a sparkly tiara that every queen took home after the festival. Today she would pass on a brand new crown, and from the looks of it, she was more than ready. She'd beaten Kitty out for the position last year, a wrinkle in Kitty's long and illustrious queen legacy, and Kitty's cronies hadn't made it easy on the girl.

"Etta here will crown our new queen. So, without further ado, let me name our new queen."

Marilyn held her breath and crossed her fingers. She wanted to be Dusty's queen. She wanted them to be the royal couple. She wanted . . .

"Kitty Leacock!"

Kitty squealed with delight. Disappointment seared every part of Marilyn's soul.

Kitty hugged her entourage, then pranced through the crowd. A group of high school boys hoisted her up onto the platform. She kissed the mayor on the cheek, then walked over and kissed Dusty fully on the lips. His eyes grew wide with surprise. She stepped away and danced toward Etta, eager for the coveted crown to grace her perfectly coiffed head once again.

"There's always next year," Gabe told her as he came to stand by Marilyn.

"Not for me," she answered, clearing the knot in her throat.

Hearing someone else named queen year after year only conjured up disappointing memories. She'd been crazy to think she'd be crowned queen. No matter how much she wanted it, deep down inside, there were just some things people shouldn't look forward to in life. And this was one of them.

"I don't think you'd like that crown," Emily piped in. "It's kinda cheap-looking. You should hold out for real diamonds."

"I pity the man," Gabe said with a humor that reached his eyes. He was starting to look like his old self. Even Marilyn felt like grinning despite the ache in her heart.

"It's not like I was expecting to win."

Gabe came to stand beside her and gently draped his arm over her shoulders. "I think you're the best."

"You're a good brother," she said, blinking back tears. "I'm glad you're home."

He hugged her. "Me, too."

After Kitty spoke a few words, the crowd began to thin out as people went on to other sights the Festival offered. Marilyn watched Dusty smile and greet folks who came by. Kitty preened and giggled, keeping her arm firmly linked through Dusty's. He didn't try to disengage himself, but Marilyn noticed he didn't act comfortable either.

"Why don't we go find Gran," Gabe suggested.

"I'm hungry," Emily piped in, grabbing Marilyn by the hand and dragging her toward the food booth.

"Marilyn, hold up."

Marilyn glanced over her shoulder as Buddy Lee

approached. He'd cleaned up today. No holey T-shirt with his overalls. Today he wore a flannel shirt with clean denims.

"Hey, Buddy Lee. Your ponies are a hit."

He nodded, a shy smile spreading over his lips. "I'm glad you like them."

"You having a good time?"

He glanced around, "Yeah, but I wanted to talk to you."

"Aunt Marilyn, I need you," Emily called from the booth.

Marilyn looked around Buddy Lee's bulk at her niece struggling with two plates. "We'll have to talk later. I should help Emily."

"Okay. Maybe we could dance later, when the music starts?"

"Sure," she called as she and Emily made their way to the picnic area.

"Are you sure you ordered enough food?" Marilyn glanced down at her niece's choices. French fries, onion rings, two burgers, and a brownie. Typical kid fare. Not the kind of diet Marilyn wanted showing on her hips.

"Daddy'll be here soon. He likes onion rings."

"So, are you settling into the school okay?"

She shrugged. "I guess. I like my teacher, Miss Summer. She's nice. And pretty."

"I didn't know being pretty was a prerequisite for a good teacher."

"Well, it's just that . . . she's a Miss."

Emily's intention suddenly became clear to Marilyn. "Oh, no, please don't tell me you have the Ruby Sue matchmaking genes."

"What?"

"You're not thinking about fixing up Miss Summer with your Daddy, are you?"

"Why not? I mean, he needs someone. He's been acting funny for a while now."

"Is that why you were acting up in your old school?"

"How else could I get him to meet some of the single teachers?"

"He thinks something's been bothering you and that's why you get into trouble. He's really concerned."

"I know. But he's so sad all the time. I just wanted to help." Emily stared down at her untouched food. "I miss Mom. I want to be a real family again."

Marilyn reached out and hugged her niece. At eleven, it was only natural that she'd want her mother. And from the depths of her soul, Marilyn understood. How many nights in her young life had she lain in her bed, a lump in her throat and her eyes burning as she tried not to cry over a mother who didn't want anything to do with her family? Only in Emily's case, a car accident had claimed her mother's life.

"Just give your daddy a little more time," she whispered.

Emily sniffed against Marilyn's shoulder. "I will. For now." She pulled back and looked solemnly into Marilyn's eyes. "But sooner or later I'm going to have to do something."

Marilyn blinked. *Shades of Ruby Sue.*

A group of girls strolled by, beckoning Emily to join them. Her beseeching look made Marilyn laugh. "Go on. I'll find someone to give your dinner to."

"Thanks." Emily jumped up, her hunger forgotten, and ran a few steps before stopping. She turned around, ran back to Marilyn, and threw her arms around her. "Thanks a lot, Aunt Marilyn."

Marilyn squeezed hard and kissed the young girl on the top of her head. "You're welcome."

"What are you and my daughter up to?"

Gabe sank down on the bench as Emily ran off, eyeing the abandoned plate of fried food heaven.

"Girl talk." No point in causing a panic when nothing had happened yet.

Gabe watched his daughter meld into the crowd. "I sure hope she settles down now that she's back in school."

"I think she will. She's focused."

Gabe stared at her, his eyes narrowed.

Marilyn laughed again, pushing the plate toward her brother. "Dig in. I know you can't stand it."

He grabbed an onion ring. "Mmm. Nothing like fair food to get your cholesterol rising."

Gabe ate and Marilyn watched the crowd, hoping her tall, dark, and handsome king would saunter up to her. Instead, she couldn't catch a single glimpse of him.

"So, what did you think of my throne creation?" Ty asked as he and Casey joined them at the picnic table.

"Remind me never to get on your bad side," Gabe quipped.

"I really hoped that you'd be up there, Sis."

Marilyn lightly waved off Ty's remark, even as another wave of disappointment hit her. "Please. After all these years I didn't expect it."

"Well, Kitty sure did," Casey chimed in. "You

know, it makes you wonder. Did you see how that woman just marched up to the stage, not the least bit surprised that she won."

"Casey, don't make a big deal out of this," her husband warned.

"Why not? I mean, who even votes for the king and queen? I didn't. Did you guys?"

That all shook their heads.

"You see what I mean? So, who votes?"

Marilyn picked up a fry and took a small bite. "I think some of the civic organizations. I know Kitty's been schmoozing them big-time for the last month or two. She didn't want to lose out again this year, especially to a younger candidate."

"Ruby Sue would know who voted. I'll ask her."

"Casey," Ty warned.

"Ty," Casey mocked his tone.

He sighed, clear who had won that battle. "Before you get all riled up, let's check out all the information."

Casey held out her hand for Ty. "C'mon. Let's do this together."

Ty grinned, the light in his eyes for Casey alone. "You got it."

Gabe chuckled as the couple strolled away. "What do you want to guess that Ty will find a very persuasive way to change Casey's mind."

"I don't know. She's got that look, like she's on a mission."

"Watch out, Paineville."

"Watch out, Queen Kitty."

"Why does she need to watch out?" Dusty asked.

Marilyn turned in surprise. "Where'd you come from?"

He tilted his head toward the mayor's booth. "Doing my public relations gig for the town." He sank down close to Marilyn. Her heart sped up as his solid body pressed against hers. A curious smile tugged at his lips. He waited for her to fill him in on the conversation. With him sitting this close, his scent surrounding her, his body heat making her blood pressure soar, she momentarily lost the use of her tongue.

"Casey raised a few questions about the king and queen thing," Gabe supplied. "No big deal."

"Really?" Dusty asked her.

"Sure," she replied, gazing up at him in a manner she was sure bordered on gawking.

"I'm off," Gabe announced, winking at Marilyn before he walked away.

"You don't seem convinced." Dusty returned to the conversation at hand.

"It's not a big deal. Casey just wondered how the royal couple was voted in."

He wrapped her hand into the warmth of his, his work-roughened fingers sending skitters over her skin. "I really hoped you'd win. I would have liked standing up there with you."

"Kitty held you up well enough."

He chuckled. "She loves being in the spotlight. This is her big moment. I think the crown is really important to her."

"Always has been."

"Maybe. But with her husband gone, I think she needs adulation from those around her to make her feel important."

Marilyn looked at Dusty, glimpsing tenderness on his face. Could she be any more attracted to this guy? Sure, he looked good, but she genuinely liked him. Heck, more than just liked him. And why?

He had a good heart. Willingly helped her grandmother. Moved to the trailer to make room for her brother in the house. Glanced into the psyche of someone like Kitty and found compassion, while all Marilyn saw were the problems from her childhood. She'd never met a man quite like him before.

Dusty made her look at life in Paineville differently. And she knew she'd never be the same woman. Especially after she left him behind.

Chapter Eleven

An early dusk fell that night. Cheery lantern lights strung around the festival grounds twinkled like stars fallen to earth. The temperature dipped, but spirits soared high. Dixie Highway took to the stage, ready to entertain visitors and townsfolk with their signature music.

Dusty glanced at Marilyn. In the fading light, shadows crossed her lovely face. He didn't know if it was the play of light or her mood. He wanted to kiss her again but held back, even though his gut twisted otherwise. Instead, he asked, "What do you say we take a turn around the dance floor?"

"Sure, but I want to ask you something, first."

"Shoot."

"You really don't mind playing king? It doesn't seem . . . silly?"

"It's a town tradition. I'm actually honored that folks consider me one of their own."

"And what happens when you leave?"

161

He searched her face. "You seem pretty sure I will."

"How can you stay? What does this place have to offer you?"

He looked out over the two-stepping couples. "Peace. Quiet. A chance to be me."

"I've been being me all my life and it hasn't gotten me anywhere."

"I disagree. You've been successful with work, I mean. You've been offered a great opportunity in Charlotte. That didn't happen just because your new boss heard good things about you. Believe me, in business you have to have an impressive sales record or this guy wouldn't want to lure you away.

"Besides that, your family loves you. The people in town, like Molly and Ben at the General Store, think the world of you. That's more than some people have."

"Maybe it's not enough."

"Only you can decide that." He sighed. "If I asked you to stay, would you?"

"Dusty, I've talked more to you about leaving than anyone else. You know how much I want to go and make a name for myself. On my own merit."

He nodded. He knew she had to try, how important it was to her. But when it came down to actually leaving, could he let her go?

He stood and offered his hand. She took it, and followed him to the makeshift dance floor. He gathered her in his embrace, swaying to the tempo of the music. He closed his eyes, inhaling the scent of her shampoo, content with Marilyn in his arms and great music coming from the band. He wanted to hold on to this moment, to treasure all the time he could get with her.

He wasn't sure just exactly when the truth of how he felt about her had hit him. He'd liked her immediately, even though she was furious with him and he thought she needed a little thawing out. As he spent days getting to know her, he found a rhythm, a comfort level he'd never experienced with another woman. And of course he enjoyed just looking at her. Who wouldn't? He thought she was the most gorgeous woman he'd ever met.

So when had this admiration of Marilyn turned into love? Oh, he'd written dozens of songs about love, adding new twists to the old tired clichés. Yet, as he held her close, rested his cheek against her hair, he realized he'd never had a clue. Not until this time and place with this woman.

A woman determined to leave. Which meant leaving him. That was a switch. Usually he was the first one to take off. But he knew she'd made her decision to strike out on her own. If he somehow made her stay, she'd never know what she missed and eventually she'd resent him for that.

So for now, he'd hold his tongue and not blurt out his feelings. Instead he hummed along to the music.

"I've never heard this song," Marilyn murmured as a new melody played.

"I know. It's new."

She looked up at him, her eyes wide. "You mean you wrote it?"

He nodded his head toward the band. "Not exactly. One of the band members got hung up on a few chords. I helped him play it out."

She stepped back and smiled up at him. "You see, you are getting your talent back. We wrote that song for Gran and now you helped the band."

He nodded, still not convinced. "I had great help both times."

"Don't sell yourself short. Before you know it, melodies will be dancing in your head."

"I hope I don't end up with a headache."

She playfully pinched his arm. "You make fun now, but I expect great things from you in no time."

"Thanks. That means a lot coming from you." The band turned the beat up a notch, enough so that Dusty had to let go. His fingers itched to touch Marilyn, but she laughed and danced to the music, so he matched her, dance step for dance step, all the while watching her flushed face.

Someday, a voice, laced in a melody, whispered in his head. *Someday.* The start of another song. He realized that without Marilyn's positive assurance and dogged persistence, he wouldn't have gotten to this point. He'd still be tuneless, afraid to try writing again. Marilyn had turned his life around. Become his muse.

He started to tell her this when Buddy Lee approached, tapping Marilyn on the shoulder. "Mind if I cut in?"

Dusty frowned but Marilyn nodded. "Sure. You mind?" she asked him.

"Go ahead." Dusty backed off and propped himself against a booth, his arms crossed over his chest, his eagle eyes never leaving Marilyn.

Someday.

* * *

Marilyn took Buddy Lee's hand in the next dance set, trying not to compare Buddy's limp grip to Dusty's firm hold on her. What an understatement. His hold on her life kept getting too tight to ignore.

"I've been trying to catch up with you all day. I wanted to talk to you."

"What's on your mind?"

"I couldn't help but notice you've been hangin' around that Dusty fellow a whole lot. He's pretty new in town. I guess I just want you to be careful."

"Buddy Lee, he's a friend. Don't worry."

"I can't help it. I see the way he looks at you and it's not friendship."

Marilyn didn't like the direction of this conversation.

"I don't want him to hurt you."

"He won't. And besides, I'm going to move soon."

Buddy Lee's face slowly turned red. "I heard that, too, and I think it's a mistake. Your home is right here in Paineville."

"And it always will be, but right now I've got to go off for a while and see life in a different city."

"Is someone making you leave?"

"Why would you think that?"

"I know you and some people don't get on. And some people, like Kitty, make you feel bad. But if you stayed, well, maybe you and me could get together. You know, be a couple."

"Buddy Lee, I appreciate what you're saying, but we're only friends. We have been all our lives. I can't see us being anything else."

"Because of Dusty?"

Oh, boy, this discussion was uncomfortably out of control. "No, I think of you like . . . a brother."

Buddy Lee's eyes opened wide, a stricken expression on his face.

"But that's a good thing. You can't have too many friends."

Taking a step back, Buddy shoved his hands in his pockets. "I don't want to be friends."

"I'm sorry, Buddy Lee."

He turned on his boot heel and lumbered away, head down. Marilyn watched, her stomach churning. She hated to hurt him like that.

Dusty appeared at her side immediately. "What happened?"

"I'm not quite sure."

Dusty dragged her to a deserted picnic table. "What did he say? You look upset."

"He wants me to stay in town. As his girlfriend."

"See, I told you he has a crush on you."

"Not anymore."

He frowned. "What did you say."

"I told him I wanted to be friends. That he's like a brother to me."

Dusty groaned. "Oh, man. The kiss of death. No guy in the world wants to hear those words."

"It's the truth."

"Maybe. But when a guy falls for a woman, he doesn't want to be her friend. Or brother."

She dropped her face into her hands. "How can I fix this?" she asked, her words muffled.

"The damage is done."

"He'll hate me forever, won't he?"

"He won't hate you, but he'll never be the same around you again."

"Great, just great." She felt like she couldn't do anything right. This night couldn't get any worse. "I'm going to the rest room. I'll be back in a minute."

Her mind whirled as she hiked across the fairgrounds. Perhaps if she'd been prepared she could have handled Buddy Lee differently. She'd never noticed how he felt about her, but she did know what it felt like to be hurt. And she'd hurt him. Maybe if she hadn't been so wrapped up in Dusty. . . .

But she was afraid Dusty had gotten hold of her heart so completely that no other man would ever take his place.

She stopped in front of the sink, splashing chilly water on her face. The cold sensation did little to alleviate her troubled state of mind. Shaking her head, she grabbed some paper towels and dabbed at her skin, then headed for the door, colliding with Kitty. Again.

"There you are. I've been looking for you."

Marilyn took a deep breath. She didn't want to deal with anything else tonight. "I was just leaving."

"No, you're not." Kitty pulled her to the center of the cramped room. "I want to give you something."

Marilyn frowned.

"Don't look so fierce. Here." Kitty pulled the sparkling tiara from her head and placed it on Marilyn's. "I want you to have this."

Marilyn reached up to adjust the weight of the headband. "Why?"

"I was thinking about how I told you I wanted to make amends. And I do. Since I've won the title so many years now, I thought you should have a turn."

"But you've always hated me."

"When we were kids, yes. You had a tight family, two older brothers to take care of you. I wanted that. But now that I'm older, I can see where friends are important. And truthfully, Marilyn, I don't really have many friends.

"Lately I've been trying to be nice, but you seem to be running away."

Marilyn blinked. Is that what Kitty had been doing? Trying to be a friend?

"I'm tired of hanging around with women who really don't want to grow up. Like earlier tonight, we were here in the ladies room and they were bad-mouthing you. I'm just tired of it all. I set them straight and I really meant it. You are a worthy adversary. How could I not like the one woman who can give me a run for my money? And I wouldn't have minded if you won the crown."

Marilyn thought back to the hurtful words she'd overheard the women saying. And realized that Kitty had said none of it. "You did that for me?"

Kitty nodded. "My folks aren't around, and since Milt died I'm alone. I see you with your family and I wish it was me. And Dusty is completely smitten with you." Kitty blinked furiously. "I want someone to look at me like that again. Like Milt did. You have it all together, Marilyn."

She had it all together? She'd never felt that way. She always thought Kitty had the dream life. Apparently not. Gran was right. Marilyn had what Kitty wanted all along.

But still, it hurt to be second, to get Kitty's hand-me-down crown. "It's okay, really. You take it back."

Marilyn tried to remove the fake diamond crown, but it tangled in her hair. "I'll be leaving town soon anyway."

"Leaving? To go where?"

"Charlotte. I'm starting a new job there." She attempted to pull a tangled lock free, to no avail.

"But Marilyn, Paineville is home."

"For you. Soon, Charlotte will be home for me. I'll adapt."

Kitty watched her with keen eyes. "Can I ask you a favor before you leave?"

"What?" Another tug on the tiara snarled her hair further.

"Will you introduce me to Dusty's friend?"

"Matt?"

"He's very handsome, in a big city kind of way."

"He lives in Nashville."

"I'm not adverse to relocating."

"But that's not home."

Kitty giggled. "I'll adapt."

Marilyn gave up wrestling with the crown and trying to follow Kitty's train of thought. She couldn't get a firm grasp on either. "Okay."

Kitty smiled brightly. "C'mon. What are we waiting for?" She led the way out of the ladies' room and beelined straight to Dusty. His eyebrows rose when he saw Marilyn firmly in Kitty's clutches.

"Don't ask," she threatened.

"This is too good. I have to." His eyes crinkled as he set his sights on the crown dangling from Marilyn's head of tangled hair.

"I gave her my crown," Kitty broke in, her voice

overly loud. "I felt it was time that Marilyn became the harvest queen. Doesn't she look wonderful?"

"Hmm. Very royal," Dusty commented.

"Not another word," Marilyn warned.

"Admit it, you like the crown."

Marilyn could just imagine the fuzz of hair puffing around the tiara. "It's silly and I can't get it off." She gave it another tug. It refused to budge.

Dusty laughed and reached over to help her out. Kitty knocked his hands down. "Don't do that. Let everyone see how pretty she looks. Look people," Kitty yelled as she straightened the tiara and Marilyn's hair. "Look at Marilyn, our new queen."

"Get me away from here," Marilyn begged Dusty.

"Sorry. Can't do. Your loyal subjects are lining up to salute you."

The curious crowd did indeed move closer. Marilyn imagined this was what it felt like to be displayed in a store window. All eyes on her whether she liked it or not.

When Matt came up beside Dusty, Kitty whispered in Marilyn's ear, all the while sporting a wide smile. "He's here. Introduce me."

Marilyn dropped her hands from her head and sighed. When had her life gotten so completely out of control?

"Matt," she called, "come meet Kitty."

He sauntered over like a rooster in a hen house, all smiles and eyeing Kitty head to toe. She held her hand out to his. "Please to make your acquaintance," she said in her best Southern drawl.

Marilyn rolled her eyes and went back to work on the tiara.

"Hold it, Sis."

Ty made his way through the crowd, Casey at his side and Gabe not far behind. Ruby Sue and the mayor joined the crowd from the other side. "Seems Casey was right to wonder about Kitty's claim to the crown."

Marilyn's hands stilled. "What are you talking about?"

"The voting was rigged," Ty answered, his face grim.

Marilyn blinked at her brother while the crowd gasped. "She cheated?"

Dusty moved close to her side and slipped his arm around her waist. She leaned into him, Ty's words knocking the steam out of her.

"I asked around," Casey told them. "It seems that the civic clubs that voted all have her circle of friends as members. Somehow they double-voted."

Marilyn looked at Kitty as she stood her ground, guilty eyes filled with regret.

"Why would you do that?"

Kitty lifted her chin. "This is all I have. It's who I am. It's who I've always been. I had to win."

Marilyn finally yanked off the tiara. "So why did you gave me the crown?"

"I felt badly about winning, knowing what I'd done."

Casey touched Marilyn's arm. "If you took out all the double votes, you won, Marilyn. Fair and square."

Marilyn looked down at the tiara dangling from her fingers. All the years she'd dreamed of what it meant to win. Of proving she wasn't like her mother. That she had integrity. All the times she wanted to be loved by the town, by the people she grew up with. Turned out, they did love her. All this time she'd been harboring self-pity. The town wasn't at fault, she was. Another member of the Banner family had finally risen to the occasion and held the reward in her hands. But the victory had come too late.

Marilyn threw the last garbage bag into the Dumpster, weary beyond words. Her arms ached from clean-up duty, but the physical work took her mind off her depressing thoughts. Her family had left minutes go and Dusty waited nearby to take her home after helping her with the dirty work.

She scanned the empty fairgrounds one last time, her eyes lingering on the stage and throne Ty had built. She could have sat up there tonight, surrounded by the accolades of the townsfolk, the pride of her family. Secure in the notion that she was finally accepted.

Banners never amounted to much and never will.

She swallowed heavily. She should have been queen to Dusty's king, but she had never gotten the chance to enjoy it. As much as she dreamed of such a moment for years, the image would be forever tarnished by her own self bias. Even Kitty's tearful apology didn't lift the pall that shrouded her.

"Ready to go home?" Dusty's quiet voice startled her.

"Yes."

She walked quietly to the truck and waited while he opened the driver's door, sliding in across the bench seat to stare out the window.

"What a night," he said, turning over the engine.

She agreed. First, Buddy Lee and then Kitty. In her

wildest nightmares she couldn't have conjured up to-night's convoluted events.

Dusty drove slowly, but before long they were in the driveway of Gran's house.

"You tired?" he asked.

"A little."

"Too tired to talk?"

"I don't know if I can do that, either."

"If it helps, I think you handled yourself with class."

After Kitty's confession, the mayor started damage control. Dixie Highway kicked in another tune, and soon the Harvest Queen drama faded. Kitty left, too wrapped up in Matt's attention to realize the full impact of her actions. Marilyn's family rallied around as they always did in crisis.

But they couldn't help her with this one. She had to sort through her conflicting emotions on her own.

She didn't want to dwell on tonight's events, so she changed the subject. "Did you and Matt come to an agreement?"

"No. He went back to Nashville empty-handed."

Stunned, she asked, "What about the band? Or the offer you couldn't refuse?"

"I refused."

"Oh, Dusty. I thought you wanted the creative freedom?"

"I do, and I'll have it. Dixie Highway wants me to produce them, but here, not in Nashville."

"How will you do that?"

"I'm seriously considering opening my own studio and starting a new label. With a limited number of musical acts. It'll be a place where I can preview my music, as well. And I'll have total control, publishing rights, and master recordings, and not answering to the executives who don't work with the artists."

"Won't that take a while?"

"The label is mostly paperwork. Building the studio will take longer, but I've already recruited Ty for the job. All I need is a local realtor to help me find the perfect house, one with a basement big enough to convert into a sound studio."

Marilyn ignored his blatant hint. "You've really thought this through?"

"Yes. And Dixie Highway wants to wait till I'm up and running, then sign on with my new label."

Marilyn glanced at his face. The lost look in his eyes had disappeared. A new sureness suffused him. He'd finally realized what he wanted and was now taking steps to achieve his goal.

She found that incredibly attractive. And immensely scary.

"So I'll be staying here in Paineville," he finally announced.

"I'm happy you figured it out."

"I sure wish you'd stay. With me."

Her heart stilled in her chest. "Why?"

"I think it's pretty obvious, but just for the sake of clarity, I'll tell you straight out. I want to see where this thing between us is going. We've got something special here, Marilyn. To be honest, I've never felt this strongly about any other woman before."

His honesty floored her. She wanted to jump up and down, clasp his face between her hands and kiss him senseless.

Until hopeless reality sunk in.

"I—I need to go. You know how important leaving is to me."

"I thought maybe that had changed."

"No, I still need to see what I can do."

She opened the truck door and slipped out before Dusty could stop her. She ran to the front door, never looking back when he called her name. If she turned and talked to him now, she knew she'd let him change her mind.

Chapter Twelve

Thanksgiving morning dawned dark and gloomy, matching Marilyn's mood. She couldn't sleep, so she slipped out of bed, and stared at the final four boxes scattered in her room. Hung over with emotion, she held her throbbing head that still ached from crying into the pillow all night. She hadn't cried this hard since her mother left.

She'd already piled the majority of her possessions, packed tight and safe, downstairs in the foyer. The last task would be carrying them all to her Caddy.

Slipping on a pair of worn jeans and a light long-sleeved shirt under a bold red sweater, Marilyn tied the laces to her hiking boots before leaving the room. She cast a final glance around, smiling as warm memories surfaced.

The memories in this house weren't hurtful. She recalled the pleasant times spent here with Emily, sharing girl talk or a rowdy pillow fight. Or soothing away tears over some childhood trauma Emily experienced from time to time.

And Ruby Sue, stalwart and loving, who had joined her here on many an occasion to chat about nothing more than life in general.

And the hours she herself had spent at the window seat, staring out over the deep, green mountains while she contemplated her future. How long had she dreamed of packing up boxes and venturing out into the big city? As she was about to do now?

Still, a nagging tie to the past kept her heart from brimming with joy at the prospect of leaving. The tie to a family that had always loved her, always supported her decisions, like today. They didn't like the fact that she was leaving, but they didn't guilt her into staying.

And what about Dusty? She shook off the thought of leaving him. Her determination had come between them. And she let it. Just as she'd let her mother's words rule her life.

She hustled down the stairs, stopping for a moment to peer into the living room. Someone had lit a fire that cast a cozy warmth into the room. She glanced at the piano, the mahogany wood gleaming in the early morning light, envisioning Dusty playing to a room full of family and friends. Shaking her head, she crossed the dining room and went into the kitchen.

In that room, Ruby Sue already bustled around in capable fashion, preparing more than one dish at a time. At the sight of her granddaughter, she sniffed her disapproval. "Cain't help you move. The family will be here at noon."

"I know, Gran. I'm not here to get in your way. I just wanted to say good-bye."

When she received no answer, she asked, "Where's Gabe and Emily?"

"They ran down to pick up Ben and Molly. Molly wanted to help me in the kitchen, but their truck's been acting up so they called for a ride." The whisk stilled in Ruby Sue's hand as she frowned at her Marilyn. "The world don't stop just because you need to up and leave, you know."

She knew Gran was upset, but the woman would never admit it. "And you've known from the start how serious I am."

"Even with all that's happened? Gabe and Emily home. Dusty courting you."

Courting? "Gran, Dusty understands why I have to go. Why can't you?"

"Because I know you, child. I raised you to be a bright young lady. But this move is just plain dumb."

"Excuse me?"

"You love it here, Marilyn. Just as much as I do. Roots are important to you. If you really wanted to leave, you could have done so years ago.

"But you didn't. This is home. And you know it just as sure as I do."

"Wow. Don't hold anything back, please, tell me exactly how you feel."

"Don't sass me, girl."

"You've managed to hit all my buttons."

"Told you. I know you."

"So you should know that I'll go anyway."

Ruby Sue scoffed, stirring the cornbread stuffing in the bowl she held with renewed vigor. The lines on her face seemed deeper, and she suddenly looked older and more tired.

"Then there's not much more I can say. We're eating at two this afternoon. You're welcome to join us if you want."

"Thanks. I love you, Gran."

"Stubborn girl," Ruby Sue muttered, turning her back to carry the bowl to the sink, her shoulders hunched in resignation.

Marilyn backed out of the kitchen. Once again conflicting emotions plagued her, but she stood tall, ready to meet her destiny.

She entered the foyer and donned her heavy jacket before picking up a box to carry out to the car. If she worked quickly, she could load up before the rest of her siblings and family friends descended. She planned on leaving well before they returned. She didn't think she could bear to see her entire family together one last time before she left.

On the last trip out, Marilyn paused, arm extended on the open trunk lid, gripping the cold metal as she looked out over the ridge that led to the trailer.

She shouldn't go there now, not even to say goodbye, not the way they'd ended things, but she knew she would.

She slammed the trunk closed and started walking in the direction of the trailer. The hard edges of aching childhood memories softened. Knowing that Dusty chose to live in her childhood home, regardless of the secrets that lingered there, made her love him even more. Somehow, the past had been easier to live with when Dusty was at her side.

She climbed the crooked stairs and knocked on the

door. After taut minutes, Dusty answered. As the door swung open to reveal him, the morning light accentuated the dark smudges curved under his eyes. Clearly he hadn't slept any better than she had. He stood under the threshold and she noticed his attire: a crisp dress shirt, dark dress slacks, and polished shoes.

"Going to a party?" she asked, trying to lighten the already tense air around them.

"Thanksgiving dinner." His eyes narrowed. "Did you need something?"

"No. I came to say goodbye."

"Why? You know how I feel about you leaving."

"And you know I have to go."

"Do you really need to go, or have you convinced yourself there are no other options?"

She rubbed her forehead. "I need to try, Dusty. For me. For years I convinced myself that people in this town thought of me as a nobody. A Banner kid."

Dusty leaned against the door frame. "Don't you get it? You are somebody. Last night should have proved that to you. The town voted for you. Your family made a united front. Isn't that what you've wanted all along?"

"Yes."

"Marilyn, the only one who sees you as a nobody is you."

Her heart began to pound against her rib cage. "That's not so."

Dusty looked puzzled. "Then what, or who, makes you feel like you aren't good enough?"

Marilyn blinked back hot tears. "My mother, okay? My own mother never thought much of her family. Just before she left for the last time, I ran out of this trailer to try and stop her. She brushed me off, like some kind of rag doll. Here I am, this little girl, asking her why she had to break our hearts. She told me right then. *Banners never amounted to much and never will. Especially Banner women.* If only you saw how she looked at me, Dusty, like she couldn't stand the sight of me. Then she got into the car and drove away.

"I never saw her again, but her words have lived in my heart and soul since the day she left. Now I need to prove to *me* that I can be successful elsewhere." She brushed at the tears on her cheeks. "So you see, I have to go."

"And I have to stay." His flat voice suppressed his disappointment, even as his eyes gleamed with an emotion she didn't dare question.

Too many memories haunted her here. She stumbled down the steps, desperately needing to escape. Before she could leave, Dusty spoke again.

"You think leaving will make you a stronger person? I disagree. Sometimes it takes more courage to stay than to walk away."

As Marilyn steered the Caddy downtown through the dissipating morning mist, she caught sight of a sign placed directly in the town square. CONGRATULATIONS DUSTY AND MARILYN, KING AND QUEEN OF THE PAINEVILLE HARVEST FESTIVAL.

She pulled to the side of the road and turned off the ignition, staring at the words, still unable to reconcile the fact that she had finally been named queen.

Tears blurred her eyes and she couldn't breathe.

Slowly, with building pressure, great heaving sobs racked her body. She wrapped her arms around her stomach, giving into the heart-rending storm. When the worst passed, she caught her breath and rested her forehead on the steering wheel, gulping in much-needed oxygen. With shaky hands, she wiped the moisture from her cheeks, all the while wondering where that outburst had come from.

Too much emotion these past few days, she reasoned. She was on overload.

Taking a cleansing breath, she turned the key.

Nothing.

Her mouth dropped open in disbelief. "Not again."

She turned the key once more—still no results.

A sudden tapping that window made her jump. She looked out to see Dusty peering in at her. She rolled the window down.

"Are you okay, ma'am?" came his concerned drawl.

"My car won't start."

"Want me to check it out?"

"Um, I appreciate the gesture, but I'm—"

He grinned. "You're afraid I won't let you leave town?"

"Worse. That you will."

He opened the door and hauled her out and straight into the warmth of his tight embrace. "No way. I couldn't stand by and let you make the biggest mistake of your life. So I followed you."

"To stop me from leaving?"

"Hopefully."

Her heart danced with joy. "Oh, Dusty, what on earth was I thinking? Leaving the one place on earth I love? Home. No matter what anyone thinks of me, good or bad, I belong."

"Glad you finally figured that out. Saves me a lot of beggin' and convincing."

She leaned back as his strong arms anchored her and she drank in the sight of him. As his gaze locked with hers, she saw an emotion she was afraid to name in case she was wrong.

"Marilyn, I thought I should let you go off to Charlotte so you could prove to yourself that you are important. Figured if I pressured you to stay, you'd regret it and in time resent me. But as I watched you drive away, I knew deep inside me that you—*we*—belong here. I decided then that I had to try to convince you to stay." A pleading look eclipsed his gaze. "I hope I'm not way off base here."

Marilyn brushed her fingers over his handsome face. Since Dusty had arrived, full of self-doubts and unsolicited advice, he not only won her heart, but made her look at herself through fresh eyes. And guess what? She wasn't lacking like she thought. No—instead she finally saw the real Marilyn, successful, happy, loved. The person Gran had tried unsuccessfully to prove existed all along.

No, she wasn't a coward. Her mother may have chosen the easy way out of her problems, but not her. If she left now, she'd fulfill the nightmare. She'd be just like her mother. She couldn't let that happen.

"Dusty, you were right. Leaving wouldn't make things better, because only regrets would follow me."

"I'm glad you finally saw the light."

"It didn't take the light. It took your faith in me."

"I've got plenty of that." Dusty tugged her closer. "I love you."

"Truly?"

"Like a song in my heart. Probably since the day you fell in that puddle and came up ready to do battle. Showed you had spirit."

"And I fought my feelings for you right from the start."

He chuckled. "What were you thinking?"

"That I love you, Dusty." And to prove it, she kissed him, with all the love she possessed in her heart and soul.